THE MASKED FATE

LUCY EWART

Contents

Chapter 1

There are three of them; one for each of us.

I stared at the blood thirsty eyes of the Kelifeo demon in front of me, its tongue flickering towards me wanting to get a taste of the blood that ran down the side of my face.

This one was a tricky little bastard. It was cunning and it knew not to come near me or my sword. Just a simple swipe of my blade and the demon will fall to ashes at my feet.

The blade was enchanted with a powerful spell. It was magic embedded into our weapons to better acquire a successful kill. It was harder for them to regenerate after a clean cut made by one of our swords. It was virtually in possible for Kelifeo demons to survive after they had been wounded by our magic wielded weapons.

It circled me, waiting for the perfect opportunity to strike. Waiting for the moment when I would lower my guard but that would never happen. I was ready and had eyes only for the Kelifeo in front of me, calculating the optimal moment when to strike, and send the demon back to hell.

From the corner of my eye I saw my best friend Gabriel fighting off another Kelifeo. He didn't have his sword in hand, and was finding it difficult to kill the bloody demon without a blade. Knowing Gabe and his combat skills he was probably holding his own. He was a fierce fighter. We both were. We were always called on special missions (like this one) because of our unique combat skills.

Gabriel and I entered into training when we were merely fourteen years of age. We were young but we were willing to learn. He always believed that the reason we were the best in our age group was because of how young we began to train. I always thought that it was because we were the best, naturally.

On my other side, I saw Kimberly (our newest novice) fighting her own Kelifeo demon. She was the same age as us, nineteen, but her gifts hadn't developed a few months ago. She was a fierce fighter, fast and cunning. Without any hesitation, I saw her decapitate the demon, bringing it down on its knees before it turned to dust. I saw the slightest trace of a smile on her face as she crouched down to examine the remains. She turned her gaze towards me and saw that I was looking at her. She waved at me, a huge grin plastered on her face. But then her expression changed into alarm.

It was just a moment of distraction but it was enough.

The demon took its opportunity and launched itself forward, slashing the front of my shirt with its razor sharp claws. A burning sensation bites my skin and I feel blood trailing down my stomach. The demon's head jerks up and sniffs at the air, smelling the newly shed blood. Bringing my foot up, I land a blow to the demon's chest, hearing the snapping of bones as my foot makes contact with its lifeless body. The blow sends it sprawling across the cave floor as it landed with a hard thump.

"Calder! Are you alright?"

Kimberly raced towards me, standing beside me with lines of worry etched on her face. Her long blond hair is disheveled and there's a jagged line of blood on her cheek. "Calder? Are you alright?" She asked again. I didn't understand why she was frantic. "We need to leave. Gabriel can take care of the last demon and-"

"No." I cut her off. The flesh wound the demon made was searing my skin; it was like a boiling pot of water had been dumped on me. My voice is clipped as I say, "We never leave a Keeper behind. Its part of the code and you'd do well in learning our laws here. You'll be stuck being a novice for years if you haven't yet learned our sacred duty. You'll never be one of us."

Without another word I ran towards my demon. Taking my sword in hand, I brought it over my head and slashed a deep gash along its abdomen. The demon let out a high shrill shriek of pain as it cowered from the wound. Kelifeo demons were one of the lower level demons. They were weak and were the most ill-bred of demons. It was odd to have come across a nest full of them. They had begun to depend on each other and seemed to have united for some reason. But this demon didn't have that any longer. We killed the rest of its nest without any major difficulty and there were just three of them left; one for each of us.

Kimberly already made her kill and Gabriel was still fighting with his demon, judging from the upper hand the demon had taken; he was struggling. I took a step towards Gabriel to aid him but stopped.

Gabriel met my eyes and thought, Kill it Cal. It's your only chance. I'll be fine.

I slightly nodded and brought my sword over my head and slashed through the demon's neck, beheading the evil creature. The body crumpled into ash only leaving its disintegrated remains behind as I sank to my knees.

"Calder!" It was Kimberly again. I don't know what it was with the new novice. She was something different that's all I knew. She's a fierce fighter yet knew nothing of our laws. "Cal? We need to get out of here. Gabriel has killed the last demon. I think-" She kneels down next to me and reaches forward to touch the wound that runs across my chest. "I think you've been poisoned."

Her eyes widen and I see the slightest glimmer of tears welling up in them. "You got a lot to learn about our world, novice." I spat the word 'novice' like it was a curse. She flinched and I got up from the ground, patting my hands on my pants to get rid of the dirt. "I'm fine. Nothing that we Keepers can't heal from."

She blinks away the now angry tears from her eyes and chews on her lip. A scowl slowly creeps onto her face and I take a step forward, not wanting to be here when she throws a tantrum.

Why is he such an arrogant ass?

"Excuse me?" I asked turning to look down at her. "What did you say?"

"I didn't say anything." She gets up from the ground and glares at me. She might not have said the thought aloud but I heard it. That's one of my gifts. I can read other's minds except for demons. They aren't considered human and thus have no indication of having thoughts at all. They are just spawns from hell created to wreak havoc on earth.

"It doesn't seem like you didn't say anything. C'mon. Amuse me. What is really on your mind?" I threaded on dangerous water but I couldn't help myself. I wanted to hear what she was thinking instead of prying into her mind.

Her eyes shot daggers at me and I smirked, waiting for her to begin.

She puckered her lips and breathed out a long sigh. "Just because you have been a Keeper for years doesn't mean that you can belittle people like me. It doesn't make you king and it certainly doesn't make you a commodity." Her eyes were burning bright with such passion and intensity that I took an unconscious step back. She rose her right eye brow at my movement and smirked. It was eerily like what my expression must have looked like when I tested her.

Kimberly glared at me (which seemed to be the thing that she loved to do when looking at me) for a few more seconds and then spun on her heel, walking to the other side of the cave where Gabriel waited.

"You both done?" Gabriel asked, sheathing his sword in the scabbard that hung on around his waist. He crossed his arms across his chest and gave me a chastising look. I loathed that look. It was the look that he gave when he was disappointed in my behavior which was often. Gabriel and I had completely opposite personalities but oddly we are the best of friends.

"Yes." We answered simultaneously. I looked at her to see that she was staring past Gabriel with a fierce fortitude. I wonder why she respects his authority but not mine. She's got spirit, I thought. I like it. It's different. Wait, what?

I shook my head from the thoughts and looked at Gabriel's bloodied and torn clothes. There was blood matted on the left side of his face and as I looked closely I saw a flesh wound above his eye-right through his eyebrow.

You alright? I asked.

Gabriel looked up at me, weariness written all over his face. Fine. Just ready to go home. We still need to report the events that occurred. File the tedious paperwork. He shrugged, waving it off. I'll take care of it.

"You sure? There's no need for you to handle all the technicalities-"

"I've got it." He cut in. His shoulders slumped forward, exhaustion washing over him. "Don't have nothing to do tonight. Might as well pour over the paperwork now rather than later. You on the other hand..." His eyes focused on me for a second too long before his eyes flickered to Kimberly.

"No. Absolutely not!" I couldn't believe that he had just insinuated that Kimberly and I...no. I wouldn't even think about what he was getting at.

Kimberly turned towards me, hands on her hips. "What the hell are you two talking about? I know it's not my place but whatever you two are talking about-can it wait? I want to go home and you two are my only ticket out." She huffed.

Gabriel and I exchanged a look. She's got spunk. She'll fit in quite well here.

I scoffed. Ha! Not with that attitude.

Gabe smiled mischievously, a glint in his eyes. I've never seen his eyes that way except when he talked about...

"You'll see." He said, my thought trailing off. Gabe smiled sadly as his eyes took on a faraway look. He was reminiscing. I knew exactly who he was remembering.

He held out his hand to Kimberly and I took his other hand. "You'll see. You won't know what hit you." I didn't have time to respond because Gabriel then began to chant a spell that would transport us back to Council headquarters. I followed suit and began to chant the familiar spell. In less than a minute I felt warmth as the magic engulfed us. Kimberly's hold on my hand tightens and I couldn't help but smile sheepishly at her.

I saw her return a small smile before we teleported out of the cave and returned home.

Uncorking a bottle of whiskey, I poured a cup for myself as I stood on the balcony of my room. There were many constellations out in the sky, each illuminating the vast plane. The Italian Council Headquarters was located in Florence, outside of the city and in the country side. At night there was just the dim lighting of the street lamps and the light from the stars and moon. There was no moon tonight and the entire place felt eerie in a way.

My nerves were heightened and I believe that the source of it was the battle with the demons this afternoon. Demons did not cluster in small groups to form a nest. It was unheard of-well not exactly. There were a few instances in our past history where Keepers had discovered different nests occupied by different species of demons. But that hasn't happened for almost a century.

There was a small knock on the glass door and I turned around, my thoughts parting for the moment. Kimberly stood timidly in the doorway, her right arm held behind her back. "May I come in, Mr. Montgomery?"

I waved her in and started to pour another glass of whiskey. Gathering the glass in my hand I offered it to her, "Drink?"

"No, thank you." She declined politely. She was acting strangely courteous and I couldn't put my finger on it. But then again, I gathered that Kimberly was the kind of person who when pushed to the limit will fight back. Hmm...like a small kitten. They were vicious creatures when you aggravated them. I should know.

"Alright then." I put the glass down and took a swig of mine. Its contents gave a slight burning sensation at the back of my throat as I swallowed. Kimberly looked at me, displeasure in her eyes. I guess she was not a fan of drinking.

"Why are you here?" I asked.

"I-" She gulped and cleared her throat. She shifted her weight from one foot to the other and turned to look over the balcony. I took the opportunity in her discomfort and read her mind. This is really beautiful. But. Ugh, I hate this. Why do I have to do this? Why couldn't I have just gone to bed like everyone else. It would have been better than to stand here with him.

"Well spit it out then." I groaned. "Why. Are. You. Here."

She turned towards me. "What's your power?"

"Excuse me?"

"What's. Your. Power."

I smiled. She definitely had spunk like Gabe said. "You know."

She rolled her eyes. "I know of one. Time traveling. It would be insane not to know since everyone talks about. But I know you have more than one. My guess is that you are a telepath."

I raised my eyebrow in amusement. "Perceptive."

Most novices don't bother to look into other Keeper's lives-as in their "powers" or gifts as we prefer to call it. Novices knew their place. They do not associate with us if they aren't spoken to and certainly do no accompany Keepers into a mission. Kimberly is rare occasion. She has barely been here for a month and she has already exceeded all the novice levels. She is one of the top novices out of forty new recruits. She certainly proved herself tonight when she took down four demons.

She has spunk.

I smiled as Gabriel's words surfaced in my mind. She definitely did. I couldn't disagree with him. There was something different about the girl standing in front of me. She wasn't hard to look at either. For the first time since this afternoon, I let my eyes wander, observing the girl before me. Kimberly had long flowing blond hair that fell in soft waves down her back. Her skin was like one of those china dolls that Gabe's older sister Jane collected; virtually flawless. She was wearing boot cut jeans that hugged her curves, a flowing purple blouse and purple heels completed her look. She was beautiful and I was familiar with what the other novices said about her.

When she looked at me, her eyes were the purest of blues like the Adriatic sea on the coast of Italy. But her eyes didn't stay blue; they changed. Sometimes they were as light as the pear trees in the valley or the color of the-

What the hell am I doing?

I shook my head, clearing my mind. "You alright there?"

"Fine." I snapped. I didn't know what it was with her. She just aggravated me to the point where I didn't have any patience for it. Then there were those thoughts of her...

"You know what?" She started. Her eyes were blazing with anger as she turned to me. "I was going to apologize to you for what I said earlier but I don't care anymore. I know I was out of line but I can't stand there while you unleash your rage and exasperation on me. I'm not like those other novices." She turned on her heels and started to walk back into the room to exit. I stared at her retreating figure, dumbfounded and fuming. How dare she talk to me like that? To me? Her superior!

I followed her out and grasped her elbow, not letting her leave. She turned and struggled against my grasp, her eyes piercing my soul as they flashed an icy blue. I let her go and threw my hands up in the air. "You need to learn where your place is. You might be better than all the other novice's this year but that does not make you better than me or Gabriel for that matter."

She scoffed. "Gabriel is different. You and him are on complete different levels in my personal opinion. He doesn't flaunt his authority like you do or belittle people. He actually has a heart unlike you."

Kimberly glared at me for a millisecond before she walked out of the room, leaving me flabbergasted as anger coursed through my veins. She slammed the door shut and I heard her let out an angry groan as I heard her heels click clack on the wooden floorboards.

"Very mature." I muttered under my breath.

I didn't know what she stirred inside of me. But it was unfamiliar territory and I did not particularly enjoy it for one bit. She was infuriating yet had her moments like when we were teleporting. Did she have a bipolar disorder or something? I don't know. But she was different.

She has spunk.

Ugh! Why wouldn't that bloody phrase get out of my head? Damn him! I need a drink.

CHAPTER 2

There was a loud knock on the door that awakened me from my slumber. I groaned and lazily rolled out of my bed, rubbing the sleep from my eyes. I focused my eyes on the nightstand where my clock rested and was furious to read that it was 4:37 A.M. I was furious at the intrusion and wondered who had the audacity to wake me up this early in the morning. The sun wasn't even on the horizon and in my standards that meant that absolutely no one should be awake at this ungodly hour. Grabbing the door knob I quickly turned it and was about to unleash my anger until I saw who was standing in the doorway. It was Elder McNolie.

"Calder. Your father has asked for your audience."

I crossed my arms over my chest and stood up straight, alert. "This early? Is something the matter? Has Gabriel been summoned also?"

McNolie rolled his eyes at me and spoke in a precise and deliberate voice. "No. He has only asked for you." He then turned on his heels and walked down the hall. I closed my door and quickly prepared, grabbing a pair of jeans and a t-shirt.

McNolie has never taken a liking towards me. Things didn't add up to my favor after I dated his daughter for a month and then ended the relationship. I received a stern reprimand for that one. Jessie apparently was heartbroken and it was my fault. After that McNolie couldn't have cared less about me. He only treated me with the slightest of respect when my father was in the same room. But my father wasn't blind to McNolie's animosity.

Walking down the corridor to the Council Chamber was eerie in the early hours of the morning. The only visible light shed was from the torch that McNolie carried in his hand. It had the whole medieval castle vibe (we actually were located inside one of Italy's oldest castles). The youngest of us Keepers have told the Council that we needed to have innovations done in the castle. We couldn't be stuck in the sixteenth century for all of eternity.

All was quiet in the eve of the night as we walked down the corridor. The only the sound was that of our heavy footsteps, echoing off the walls. From the corner of my eyes I saw our shadows flicker on the walls as we passed, bleak and unsettling. I hated walking down these corridors at night because of the chills that ran down my spine. There were things that went bump in the night, things that I hunted and killed.

I checked my watch on my wrist and read that it was now four fifty-two. McNolie opened the tall, looming door to the chamber and he bid me to go in first. As I walked into the chamber I saw that my father was the only one up on the dais. Behind me, McNolie began to close the door, creaking until it thundered closed in the empty room. I found it odd that Elder

Montehue was not present for the audience. It made me wonder what my father wanted to talk to me about.

"Calder." He said. I walked towards the dais to the right side of the room and kneeled before him. I bowed my head before I stood up and looked into my father's weary eyes. He was tired. Who wouldn't be at this hour? There were dark circles rimming his eyes from lack of sleep and I wondered if he had even gone to bed tonight. As I stood in front of him, I started to realize that this wasn't Keeper business that I had been summoned to. No, this was personal.

"What is going on with you and Kimberly Amato?" He asked frankly.

I was taken aback and didn't know how to process that question. There was no forlorn warning. Nothing to indicate that this was the topic of conversation we would be having. "What do you mean? There is absolutely nothing going on between us."

"That is the exact opposite of the emotions I felt from here last night."

Oh. So it was that. My father's gift was empathy. He could feel other's emotions when they were at their highest intensity. Reading humans emotions was easier than reading our kinds because humans were vulnerable, and they did not have full control of their emotions, not like we did. Kimberly was still a novice which meant that she had not yet learned to control her feelings.

"What did you feel?" I was curious. I wanted to know what her emotions were. Was she angry? That would be my first guess after the way that she left last night.

"Strangely, it was confusion."

"Confusion?"

My father then did the oddest thing. He smiled. He actually had a small smile on his face and his eyes glimmered with mischief. It reminded me of the look that Gabriel gave me yesterday. "She's confused about how she feels about you. Not to mention that she was also seething with anger." He smirked at that admission. "Tell me. What on heaven's name did you do to the girl?" I opened my mouth to respond but then he waved his hand to silence me. "Never mind."

He took a deep breath as he touched the wedding ring on his finger. "There was also admiration for you at the same time." His voice was low and gruff, lost in another time. He looked back at me and added, "Just like your mother."

I didn't know what to say. My father didn't talk about my mother much. She was murdered when I was just a baby. I was two when a Veilno demon left her mutilated body on the Council steps. My father hunted down the bloody beast and killed it himself. He was never the same again after her death. At least, that is what I heard from other Keepers. I was too young to remember who she was. All I had were photographs and stories that were told when I was younger. It was odd for him to have mentioned my mother. The only story he ever revealed was about her death. Even then, the details were always exact and no emotion could be conveyed from the tale.

This time it was different. He wanted to talk about her. I could see it in his eyes how he longed for me to know who she was and the feeling was mutual. Maybe he thought that it was the right time for the conversation. The thing that I didn't understand was how he had compared Mom to Kimberly.

I was completely engrossed in my own thoughts that I didn't even notice that my father was already gone from his seat. I saw his figure striding past the back exit as silent as a spirit who haunts the very halls where it died. My father was like a ghost, silently going day by day without the love of another.

I didn't know how much that was true until now.

"You okay, Cal?" Gabriel asked after our grueling training session. My blond hair was matted to my forehead in sticky clumps as I ran my fingers through it; bad idea. My hand came away covered with a sheen of sweat and I grabbed a towel to wipe it clean. I needed a shower.

"Fine. Why?"

Gabe wiped his face with his spare towel and casually wrapped it around his neck. "You seemed out of it today. Anything you want to talk about?"

He knew something was wrong and he was right. I just didn't want to talk about it. There were so many thoughts running through my mind that I didn't know where they began and ended. I was thinking about my mother and father. There was a sense of longing to know how they met. How they fell in love. Was it like Gabriel's parents? Their story was "so romantic" as a lot of Keeper girls liked to say. I was also thinking about Kimberly...

"Calder." Gabriel said, waving his hand in front of my face. I snapped my attention back to him and saw the concern in his eyes. "What is going on?"

"Nothing." I said as I began to pack my stuff back into my duffle bag. "I just got stuff on my mind. Nothing to plague you about."

"Would one of those things be a girl?"

I turned around to see a grin on his face. I scowled. I hated when he guessed right. "So I am right, I see." Gabriel sat down on one of the empty benches of the gym and I followed. "She's got you like a fish trapped in a net."

"Not so much like a net. Probably more like a spider's web."

Gabriel chuckled. "So now she's a venomous vip-"

"No." I cut in laughing. "No, she's not. I don't know. There's just something about her. My father told me something today and it just keeps replaying in my head, man."

"Hmm…" I hated when he said that. It meant that he was thinking and with Gabriel it was never good to think especially when it concerned matters of the heart. "Maybe, you should just wait it out. See how things go from here. You haven't even had a conversation with her that doesn't turn into a barb."

I chuckled. He was right. Every time Kimberly and I talked it somehow turned intense with both of us walking away fuming with anger. Wasn't last night evidence of that? Kimberly just stirred something inside of me, something alien and foreign.

Speaking of alien and foreign, there was something that bothered me about last night's mission. "Hey, did you notice how there was a nest of them last night?" I asked.

Gabriel's hand involuntarily went to touch the scar on his left eyebrow. It wasn't as noticeable as he thought but when he stood under direct light a person could see the small scar that now spliced his eyebrow. "Yeah, I've been meaning to talk to you about that. I wrote it in the report last night. I was thinking of also telling my father just to take matters cautiously."

I nodded. "I agree. We should tell the Council. It would take a few days for them to read the report. It would be better for them to know now then in a few days." I pushed myself up from the bench and began to gather my belongings. "I'll meet you in the chamber in an hour. Sound good?"

"Sounds good. See you in an hour, Cal." Gabriel gathered his duffle bag and headed towards the door but then he abruptly stopped and turned around with a sly smile on his face. "Try being nicer to her. Maybe that will help." He said. I didn't have a chance to reply because the next moment he was swiftly out the door, softly chuckling as he walked out of the gym.

Be nicer? He wanted me to be nicer to Kimberly. Was he insane? I thought I was being nice to her. She's the one who takes the initiative to aggravate me at any chance she gets. She also thinks that she is above everyone else when she is just a novice and doesn't respect her elders. She has no respect for anyone else but herself...wait that's not true. She respects Gabe but I don't know why she doesn't respect me. What did I ever do to her?

Breathe.

I took a deep calming breath. I needed to center myself and not let my emotions get the best of me. I hated to admit it but Gabriel was right. I needed to be civil when I conversed with her. But what if being nice killed me in the process?

I chuckled quietly. "What am I getting myself into?"

Gabriel and I stood in front of the Council members in the chamber, their gazes set on both of us. They were seated behind the long, dark mahogany desk in their own rightful seats which were long ago chosen by the powers that gifted our kind. There are seven families chosen for each council around the world depending on who were the very first families to have settled in the region and receive the gift and honor of protecting time. In the Italian Council both our fathers' descendants had been one of the first seven people given the sacred duty to protect the essence of time.

Gabriel's father, Elder Montehue, was the head of the Italian Council. My father, Elder Montgomery followed after as his second in command should Montehue be absent or killed in battle. On my father's left sat Gilvonie and Cieu who were deadly skilled fighters. Many people in the council whispered that Gabriel and I would one day be legends as they are. It wasn't a secret that we were well on our way to be known around the world. When Gabriel and I visited Australia last summer as part of one of our missions - by the end of our stay our names were praised and known all throughout the continent. By the time we arrived home we were welcomed and congratulated for our feat. We killed ten Velbin demons single handedly. It was no easy task because Velbindemons have poison in their claws that paralyzes to the touch. We had to wear armor to protect ourselves from the demon which we weren't trained in. But we managed nonetheless.

On Elder Montehue's right sat Mcnolie (who hated my guts), Rocovik, and finally Marrino. Rocovik and Marrino were extremely intelligent and cunning Keepers. They used their mind to assess a situation rather than expending their energy. Rocovik has the gift of predicting the future in a matter of seconds.

He could will his mind to look forward in time for a minute or a month or years. His gift was the reason he was often attacked by demons when he was a child and the scars to prove it. When I first met Rocovik, I couldn't stop starring at the scars that marred his face. They were angry slits that ran from his left eye to his chin. I was only fourteen and wondered what had caused his face to be marred. As the years passed, I realized that his scarred face made him who he is today. Rocovik is a kind soul who is loved by his wife Victoria for who he is no matter the scars that graced his body. He was also a deadly and fierce fighter. I've only seen him once in the heat of battle and it truly was a sight to behold.

Marrino's gift is psychometry. He can read information by touching an object. He can know absolutely everything from a person's belongings like their past, present, and future. His gift is useful in battle when a demon drops a valuable possession (it rarely happens) from the human it has killed or is being held captive. If we find an object we report immediately to Marrino and in a matter of minutes we know whether the person is alive or dead. If they are alive, Marrino knows their whereabouts and we quickly form a rescue unit to safely bring the human home to their family.

Humans are easy prey for demons, especially those who have no homes or are alone in the dark of the night. Then there are some Keepers who befriend humans which make them easier targets for demons. Demons enjoy causing misery and what better way to provoke a Keeper. It's not a smart move on their part because we always annihilate the evil creatures. But it is an unwritten rule that we stay as far away from humans as possible.

It is better for their safety. It isn't forbidden to befriend humans but it is forbidden to love them. It's a rule that Gabriel is familiar with...

"Calder!"

I snapped out of my revere and faced my father's troubled gaze. His eyes were set in wide fury, his face flushed with anger. "If you cannot pay attention then I will have to ask you to leave, son."

"I offer my sincerest apologizes." I bowed my head and kneeled down, waiting for the Council to accept my act of contrition.

"You may remain, Calder." Elder Montehue said. "But please, mind your focus."

"Yes, sir." I looked over at Gabriel as he thought, What were you so engrossed with?

Nothing of importance.

He looked skeptical but turned his attention back to the council. They were in hushed tones, whispering to each other and keeping an eye on us at the same time. Gabriel shuffled his weight from one foot to the other, waiting for the Council's decision on the matter. I was at a lost considering that I had blanked out for the duration of the meeting.

Suddenly, the chamber was silent as if someone had cast a silencing spell on the room. But no one had done such a thing. The Council was ready to deliver their verdict as I stared into my father's cold unyielding eyes. Elder Montehue held his son's gaze for a moment too long before his eyes flickered to mine. He cleared his throat and ruffled the papers in front of him causing the sound to be deafening.

"I am pleased that both of you took the necessary precautions to come and speak to us about what you experienced last night." Elder Montehue began looking over to his son as his eyes bright with respect. His eyes then roamed to mine and he gave me a small smile and the same look of respect in his eyes. At that moment I wanted to be able to read Montehue's mind but I couldn't. It was against our code to use our powers on any council member. I wouldn't be able to try to read his mind even if I did try. There was some sort of veil covering their deepest thoughts; a spell of some sort.

I knew that for a fact.

I had only been here for a few weeks with my powers raw and out of my control. Somehow, I started to read into Elder Rocovik's mind and the next thing I knew my head felt like it was splitting in half. I started to scream in agony and I dropped down to the floor, my hands covering my ears. Rocovickwas by my side in seconds and as soon as he touched me the pain stopped. I think that he realized that I was reading his mind and began to weave a spell insure my safety. I couldn't read his mind or any of the other council members since then.

"We have concluded," Montehue commenced, shuffling the pieces of parchment in his hand and passing the papers to my father, "that the matter is not urgent and in need of immediate investigation." I looked over at Gabriel's tense jaw and recognize the retort on his tongue. Don't, I thought loudly in my mind, focusing it towards Gabe. Gabriel flinched and gave me a sidelong glance. Don't do anything rash. We'll talk about this later. You think it's a bad decision?

Yes, I have a terrible feeling about last night. Something is happening, Cal. Something beyond our comprehension. I can feel it.

"Although the matter is of no urgent need, we have decided to alert the rest of the Keepers about the occurrence." Elder Montehue continued. "We will organize a meeting with all Keepers within the next day and inform them of the recent change of demonic activity. If any members should come across the same incident I will notify them to come straightly to the both of you. You will then come straight to us. Is that understood?"

Gabriel and I exchanged a silent nod before we said, "Yes, sir."

"Good." Elder Montehue said. He rose out of his chair, taking the pieces of parchment in his hands. "You may be excused."

One by one, each member of the council began to rise, following Montehue out through the back entrance in silence. Gabriel and I headed out of the chamber silently as it would seem to any unwanted eyes and ears. Gabe was concerned about the verdict and we had the conversation telepathically as to not gather unwanted attention. It couldn't wait until we got behind closed doors. Gabriel wanted to talk now.

What is wrong with my father? Gabriel exclaimed. He was furious about the decision the Council had made. Is he insane? Something is definitely happening and for him to not take action-

Will you be reasonable? I interjected. He is just taking necessary precaution. We don't have enough evidence and even if your father agreed with us he might have been overruled. He isn't the only one who votes.

I know, He sighed. But something is going on. I can feel it. I don't know how to explain it but something in my gut is warning me about this.

We stopped right outside my corridor, Gabriel stumbled and I held out my hand for help but he shook his head. I lowered my voice and asked, "You alright? Is something else bothering you than-"

"No." He said absentmindedly touching the chain around his neck. Ah. So it was her. He was thinking about her again. "Look, I'll see you later. I'm going to go and try to find more information about this."

"Yeah, okay. Sounds good." I said. When Gabriel began to think about the only girl he's ever loved it was no use getting through him. It also didn't help when he wore a chain that she had given him for his birthday. I didn't get why he held on to her existence. She was a mortal. She would never fit into our world. Gabriel knew this. He knew that if he went back to see her she'd be in mortal danger. That's the only thing that kept him from returning to his home.

Gabriel was already down the hall before I got an idea. "Hey, Gabe!" I called. He turned around, his eyes glazed over as he was stuck in a memory from long ago. "Tonight. Think you can handle a few drinks down at Gilroy's?"

He smirked. "I think I can handle more than you can hold down any day."

"That would be true if alcohol had any effect on our bodies." I called. Gabriel chuckled and began to walk towards his corridor at the end of the hall. His footsteps echoed along the walls until I was safely back inside my dark and quiet room. I looked at the clock on my nightstand and read 6:17 P.M. One look at my rumpled and disheveled bed was enough to coax me into a few hours of lethargy. I slowly sunk into the mattress, letting sleep engulf me after a long day.

CHAPTER 3

T he blaring speakers drummed with a steady pulse underneath the wooden floorboards.

There's a cacophony of sounds blending together in the highly esteemed club – from the techno music the dj was spinning to the conversations being held all around. Drink glasses clattered a few feet in front of me as a waitress dropped her tray. Bodies swarmed around her, making her disappear from my line of vision. I could barely hear Calder, with all the noise surrounding me. It was difficult to tune out everything and not let my gift over power my senses. Not only was I graced with the gift of time traveling but I also had heightened senses and an immense power over magic wielding.

Calder sat next to me with a bottle of whiskey in his hand as he talked about girls, a topic that was not up for conversation as he knew. If our bodies could retain the effects of alcohol like a normal human body, then Calder would be beyond wasted by now. He had downed two martinis, two bottles of red wine, and four beers, yet he wasn't the least bit buzzed. I, on the other hand, had only had two glasses of red wine. What was the point of drinking when you couldn't get drunk? There were days when I wished I could do that very thing but our bodies self-healed very quickly and wouldn't retain the harming effects that alcohol contained. It just flushed it out; never allowing us to get drunk.

Calder kept on prattling about girls, a subject that he found entertaining to talk about. He took amusement in picking out a random girl in the crowd and begins to judge who she was based on her appearance. When his assumption of the right girl for me was made he'd press me to go and talk to her. He always pushed it, always forgetting my reason for not being with anyone else. He didn't understand. No one did.

I felt out of my element at Gilroy's. This wasn't my usual go to place and I didn't understand why I ever agreed to come with Cal tonight, knowing his usual behavior. I guess it was just impulse – not paying much attention to what the evenings events might hold. There was a couple in the seating area next to us, completely engrossed in nothing but themselves. A huge smile spread over her lips as the guy said something flattering and she leaned in to kiss him. I looked away, thinking of what could have been – what I could have had. I wondered how things would be different if she was here with me. Would she have accepted what I am or would she have turned me away? I wondered how she was and longed to see her, if only for one more time.

"Man, lighten up." Cal said punching my arm. I snapped out of my thoughts and turned towards my friend. "You need to loosen up. Look over there," he hung his arm around my shoulder, beer bottle in hand, and pointed to the entrance where

Tracy Vanhoul had just walked in with two other new novices; one of them was Kimberly. "Ah, shit!" He said as soon as he saw Kim. He proceeded to call the waiter over but then stopped. My eyebrows knitted together in puzzlement and he waved off my inquiry. "Well, never mind that. Tracy has a thing for you, believe me I know." He wiggled his eyebrows and I snorted. "Why don't you go over and talk to her. Make small talk. What do you say?"

He might not have been drunk but he surly acted like he was. "I think I'll pass. Why don't you go and talk to Kimberly." I nudged him with my elbow which caused him to spill a bit of the bottles contents on his pants.

He grimaced. "Thanks, bro."

I chuckled. "Sure. Anytime." I stood up and started to head where Kimberly stood, aimlessly looking around her surroundings. "I'll be right back."

"If you bring her here...." His voice was drowned out by the blaring music that thundered throughout the club. I made my way to Kimberly, side stepping through the sweaty bodies of the massive crowd. Calder may be pissed about what I was about to do but I couldn't care less. He's never taken my feelings into account when it came to my love life so why should I think of his? He'd thank me for this later.

I couldn't see the reasoning behind his dislike towards Kimberly. I've talked to her a few times during the novice training sessions and she had quite a character. She had spunk, as I perceived it. Not only was she a nice girl but she was also strong and fearless, taking every challenge thrown at her with grace and persistent execution. She was the kind of girl that I'd think would be a match for my best friend. They were both relentless fighters who took their duty in the highest regard imaginable, but then again, their personalities were polar opposites.

"Gabriel!" Kimberly called as soon as she saw me. She weaved through the crowd and met me half way in the middle of the dance floor. "It's so good to see a friendly face!" She screamed over the music. "I honestly don't know what I've gotten myself into!"

I leaned in closer to her ear and said, "You and I both. If it wasn't for Calder I wouldn't be here right now." I started heading back to the open seating area where Cal waited but Kimberly grasped my wrist. "No! I can't go with you. He hates me. I'll just go and find Tracy."

"You're joking! C'mon, it'll be fine." I grabbed her wrist and pull her through the crowd, avoiding the spots where it was impossible to get through. By the time that we got to the seating area, there were two girls sitting on either side of Calder in an indecent manner.

"Gabriel, good of you to join us!" He said in mock merriment. "Oh, and you brought dear Kimberly with you."

Kimberly's body became rigid next to mine. Her eyes held a hint of disappointment but she quickly pulled a mask over her features, hiding the fact that she was hurt. I was baffled by Calder's erratic behavior and even more confused as to the reason for his sudden change in character. "What the hell is the matter with you?"

"What?" He asked acting oblivious. "Can't a guy have some fun? There's plenty of room for you to join, right girls?" The girls nodded their heads in vigor and licked their lips, inviting me to join them.

I rolled my eyes and crossed my arms over my chest. "You are unbelievable." Kimberly was staring straight at Calder and getting daggers shot at her by the two girls that were now almost sitting on top of his lap. I didn't know the girls; they weren't Keepers. He should know better – initiating contact with humans wasn't forbidden but it kept them out of danger. How many times had he told me that?

"I'm going to head out, Gabe. I'll see you tomorrow at training." Kimberly said, casting a disappointed look at Calder.

"Hey, wait!" I called after her. She stopped and I signaled her to wait. I turned back to Calder to see his arrogant demeanor fall. I was seething with anger as I stared into the eyes of my best friend. It was all an act, a stupid and fickle act where he didn't care who was hurt, especially when it involved Kimberly.

"Gabriel, I didn't mean-"

I held up my hand to silence him and gave his new friends a cold look that made them scurry in a matter of seconds. "What is your problem? Why do you push her away? What is it? Are you afraid of what might actually happen?" My voice was loud and I felt like I was gaining an audience as the people around us stopped and stared. Stepping closer to Calder, I lowered my voice and said, "You're lucky. You can actually possibly find someone to love and who will love you if only you'd let them in. Some of us aren't that fortunate."

"You think that Kimberly loves me?" He scoffed. "Yeah, right. Love is just an illusion of a hopeless heart. I don't need anyone to love me."

I shook my head. "You're wrong. One day you'll see how much that statement is wrong, and when you do I hope that there is someone who has been waiting for you to realize it." I said, starring into his cold blue storming eyes. He was livid.

"Whatever you say, Gabriel. I forgot how much of an expert you are on the subject. But wait, you can't even find someone who is of your kind to love so I don't think that you have much room to talk."

I clenched my jaw, biting at the inside of my mouth by accident. He had absolutely no right. He had no right to bring Gwen into this. I didn't even know who this person in front of me was. I didn't know why he was acting like this.

"I hope you enjoy your time with your new friends. Come find me when you've gotten your act together. Because right now, I don't even know who you are." I spat, turning on my heels and heading towards a wide eyed Kimberly.

"What is his problem?"

I shrugged. "Don't know. But whatever it is, it's not him."

She scoffed. "Yeah, right. I think that that guy back there is exactly who he is."

I'm an idiot.

I screwed up. How could I have been a stupid, pompous, arrogant, ass? I have no excuse – I couldn't blame it on the alcohol since I don't get drunk. No. The things that I said were made by own volatile words. Gabriel was pissed off at me – that much I knew. The only reason that I could give him to loathe me was bringing up Gwen and I'd done just that.

"Hey, baby," the girl on my lap said trying to sound American, "you wanna go back to my place?" Her hand slid down my inner thigh, edging closely to my bulge. I grabbed her hand and she moaned thinking that I'd want to continue her entertainment, but I pushed her off of me and stood up, taking my jacket and slipping it on. I wasn't in the mood to play anymore. She pouted her red stained lips and folded her arms across her chest.

"Sorry, love. Got other places to be." Striding towards the exit, I didn't look back at Jenna – at least, I think that was her name. God, I couldn't even remember her damn name! I'm a stupid, condescending idiot. I wouldn't blame him if he'd never talk to me again. Then there was Kimberly. I'd just acted like I couldn't care less about her but that's the opposite of what I felt. I don't know why I did what I did. But I can't take it back now. I just have to find a way to make things right again.

The chilly November air bit at my skin for only a split second - as I walked out of Gilroy's and started the long walk home. Outside the club there was a long line that rounded around the corner, freezing bodies waiting to get inside. I didn't feel anything as I walked the empty dim lit streets. Our bodies just adapted to whatever temperature beset our environment. It took the necessary precautions to better equip our surroundings by generating either warmth or coolness depending on what the weather was like. It's like being your own heating or AC machine – it had its perks.

The streets were bleak and barren, giving the night an ominous and dreary vibe. I kept to the shadows, avoiding the questioning gazes of the people who sat outside their windows, watching the night like wide-eyed owls.

I kept thinking about the questions that Gabriel had thrown at me, analyzing each and every single one until I could come up with an answer. The first was: What is your problem? Well, I didn't exactly know what my problem was. I don't know why I did what I did. Moving on…Next question was: What is it? Again, I didn't know. It was just out of impulsive. I didn't want Kimberly to come over to where we were. The next thing I knew, two girls were seated in my lap, acting rather promiscuous. The third and final question that he asked was: Are you afraid of what might actually happen? Was I afraid? I didn't know the answer to that question either. What exactly was love anyway? I meant what I said to Gabriel. Love was for the hopeless heart; a person who has a desire to be loved by someone, who needs that to survive. I've been fine all these years. I didn't need anyone. I certainly didn't need Kimberly in my life to make it any better.

What are you afraid of?

What was I afraid of…I don't know. There was an answer for everything. There was a theory for every aspect of life. My theory of my fear of love…? Maybe, I was afraid of the same unfortunate event that happened to my father. I don't believe that I could live with myself if the one person I loved died. How horribly unbearable to live for centuries with the burden of a broken heart…no. I wouldn't even put myself in that position. I'd rather live a long and lonely life (not saying that my life was lonely because I didn't have a lover) than to possibly lose the love of my life; my soul mate.

I needed to apologize to Gabriel. I shouldn't have said the things I said about Gwen. It was a touchy subject whenever she was mentioned or he thought of her like he was earlier today. Gwen was his best friend since they were in first grade. They met at the lake where he used to go to when he was a kid. He was bit by a snake and she found him and ran to her mom to tell her about the boy– from that day on a bond formed that turned into a friendship which then grow into something more. When he found out about his gift he couldn't tell her because of the rules (mortals cannot know – under any circumstances, what we are). He knew for a few months before he had to leave and the secret burned at the edge of his tongue. He wished - or should I say wishes that he could have told her what was going on. He wishes that he could have said goodbye. But he couldn't even do that. His parents wouldn't allow it – sure that he could not go through the goodbye without giving her an explanation as to where he was going.

His feelings grew from then on. Gabriel realized that he was in love with her after months of being apart from her. What's that saying...absence makes the heart grow fonder? Well, that was exactly what happened to him. The only thing he has to remind him of Gwen is the chain he wears around his neck. It has a picture of the two of them on their final days of being together. They are at a fair in the small town they grew up in and he's giving her a piggy back ride. They look happy together without a care in the world except for that brief moment of time captured by the camera.

Gabriel's longing for Gwen is another reason as to why I don't bother with love. Why would I want to feel the possible pain of heart break? Isn't it better to see others do mistakes than to do them yourself? I think so. Love is just a fallacy; a way to hold on to something so that you feel needed and wanted. I was perfectly capable of taking care of myself. I've been doing well for the last nineteen years.

But then, why did I feel like something was indeed missing?

CHAPTER 4

The next day at the novice training session, I walked into a snake pit.

Well, that's how it seemed to me anyway. Gabriel and Kimberly were huddled in a corner of the room laughing about something. The moment that I walked in they looked up and quickly averted their eyes. It made me feel even worse about my transgression. I clenched my jaw and walked towards the men's locker room where I tossed my gym bag onto the bench as anger boiled inside of me.

Closing my eyes, I centered my being and focused on Gabriel's mind. In a matter of seconds I was able to get a clear connection of his thoughts.

Perhaps I'm being too hard on him. Maybe I should be the one to go and talk to him – tell him I'm not angry at him. But then again, I believe that he should apologize for the things he said. What he needs to do is talk to Kimberly. Poor girl is hurting because of him. He can be so blind. I really wonder why I am even friends with him…He needs to learn that he can't be selfish any longer. There are people to put into consideration other than just himself. There are young novices that look up to the both of us and he is setting up a bad example of the rest of us. What would they think?

A loud bang resonated throughout the room and I snapped my eyes open to see what the commotion was about. Standing a few feet to the right of me was Lucas Icort. He was the same age as me and a well-known heart breaker at least that is what the girls said. But personally, I didn't know the guy and never once gave him a second thought. He wasn't as great a fighter as Gabriel or I but he was alright in his own element, which was Pyrokinesis. He had the power to manipulate the element of fire to his own will. It came in handy when he was assigned to a rescue mission. In a matter of minutes, every demon within the premises would be extinguished with only the dust of their remains to indicate their being.

"Hey, Cal, shouldn't you be out there? Gabe's already started training." He said as he made his way towards the exit.

"Yeah, I'll be there in a minute."

Quickly, I changed into black basketball shorts and a blue t-shirt. When I emerged from the lockers, the group had already finished with the stretching part of training. Gabriel shot me and indignant look and said, "Now, today you each will be pairing off with a Keeper." There was a low murmur of exchange between the novices as he said this information. "I have assigned each of you so don't worry about choosing a partner." There were sighs of disappointment from a few girls and Gabriel couldn't help but smile and knowing smile. He took out a paper from his shorts pocket and began to read of the pairs. I couldn't believe that he hadn't run through today's session with me. After all he and I ran this class. It was one of the many privileges/assignments we were given.

You're forgetting about how you were an ass last night, my conscious scolded.

"Jessie you'll be with Grant. Stacey and Lily; you'll be working together..." The two girls high-fived and Gabriel smiled. "Nole you and Tori will be working together. Ms. Fields and Mr. Collins; Kimberly you'll be with..." Shit! Not me. If he paired me with her I was going to- "You'll be with Lucas."

Kim's face held a trace of disappointment but she brightened up once Lucas caught her attention and waved at her. She smiled back and averted her eyes after holding their gazes for a moment too long. Lucas ran hand through his hair sheepishly and dug his hands in his pockets.

What the hell? Out of curiosity I took a peak into Lucas' mind and was astounded.

I hope I don't act like a dim wit. Don't want to turn her off after just meeting her even though, I've known who she was for the last couple of months. She's beautiful and an excellent student. I'm going to show her how to control her power. Gabe made a good choice by pairing us off together. I am the only one in this room who can teach her balance and control through meditating. I wonder who Beth will be paired off with. The only other logical partner would be Calder since he'...

I didn't need to hear more. I knew exactly where he was going, but why did Gabriel not pair Kimberly off with me? I would have been a better suitor than Lucas any day. He could teach Beth to the basic principles of meditating. Kimberly was far more advanced than that. He was just going to waste her training session.

But why didn't Gabriel pair me off with her? Oh, that's right, because I'm an ass.

He resumed reading names of the list and to no surprise to me - I was paired with Beth Hamilton. Gabriel on the other hand wasn't paired with anyone because there were an odd number of people in training today. I noticed that Holly Grey was missing and made a mental note to ask Gabriel about it later. Since Gabriel did not have a partner he would resume the role of teacher and watch the novices train with their partners.

Beth timidly walked towards me and stood in front of me, all wide eyed and innocent. She was a cute kid. At only fifteen (and the youngest novice in the room) she was learning to master her gift in telekinesis - the same power as Kimberly. She was only five feet tall and petite but was a fierce little thing. I saw the way that she admired Kimberly and have heard her say that she wished she could be that confident and passionate.

I looked across the room to where Kimberly and Lucas sat cross legged and felt a pang in my chest. I shook the feeling off and wondered what it was. Looking back at Beth, I saw her brown eyes looking at me with respect and admiration. It made me think that Gabriel was right - no surprise there.

Breathing out a long sigh, I said, "So, you ready to train, kid?"

She nodded her head, her eyes brightening with glee. I led her to a corner of the room where we could practice alone without any interruptions. Telekinesis took immense energy and concentration, something that was not mastered over night. Even with my telepathy - there are rare occasions that I cannot control my power. When someone's emotions are on high, my telepathy is sensitive and can pick up on the person's thoughts like radar.

"So what do you want me to do?"

I thought for a moment and then said, "I want you to," I focused mind and in seconds materialized a book in my hands. All Keepers had a small amount of magic in us that we could materialize small things. Our magic was nowhere near Gabriel's – where he could materialize furniture or a car if he wanted to.

"I want you to levitate this book from the ground; only a few inches. From then on I will further instruct you on what to do."

"Okay." She bit her lip. "I can do that."

We took our seats opposite each other on the mat and I placed the book in between us. Beth bit her lip and closed her eyes, taking deep and steady breaths. Slowly, she began to bring her hand up and the book – after some struggle – began to levitate from the mat. It was shaky and beads of sweat formed on Beth's forehead and upper lip.

"Okay, good. You are doing good, kid." She smiled but her eyes remained shut. "Now, focus every fiber of your being into moving the book to your left. Forget about your surroundings, let them go and fade into the background. It is only you and the book. Relax. Continue to take deep and steady breaths."

She followed instructions and after a few minutes, the book began to slowly move to the left. "Yes! Good. You are doing well, Beth. Keep your focus. Do you feel the magic coursing through your body?"

"Yes."

"How does it feel?"

"It feels hot like everything is on fire around me..."

"Keep your focus. It's alright." I said as quietly as possible. I didn't want to break her center as she continued to levitate the book while moving it. But her strength was diminishing and in turn the book began to falter. There was a loud crash like a dish had been thrown at the wall and Beth jumped – the book soaring to the left and hitting the wall with a heavy thump. Beth was shivering and mumbling, "I'm sorry, Calder. I'm so sorry...."

"It's alright, Beth. It wasn't your fault." I turned my attention to where Kimberly and Lucas stood, broken pieces of glass beneath their feet. Kimberly buried her face in her hands and Lucas rubbed her back in small circles. Everyone in the room had stopped with their training and were now looking at the two of them with questioning eyes. Gabriel walked towards them with a clipboard in hand and began to take notes – probably on what had occurred.

"Are you going to go and see what is going on," asked Beth.

"I-I..." I cleared my throat. When did I become so tongue-tied. Maybe it was because I was in front of Beth and I didn't want the kid to see me at my worst. "I think Gabriel can handle it."

She nodded. I looked over her features and she was looking a little pale. "Beth, are you alright?"

"Mhm...I just feel weak..."

She proceeded to stand up but her knees gave out on her and I steadied her until she was balanced. "It's alright. We are done for today, kid. Practice is almost over. I'll take you to your room, sound good?"

"Yeah. I'm sorry. I wish I could be stronger like Kim..."

"Hey," I said, kneeling down and looking her right in the eyes, "Don't go and compare yourself to others, kid. You will be strong one day. But it takes practice. I'll help you if you are committed."

"You would?" She asked with hopeful eyes.

"Absolutely."

"Alright, class!" Gabriel said, calling everyone to attention. "Training is over for today. Very good start everyone. I'll see you all back here Wednesday. You are dismissed."

I stood up and took Beth in my arms. She was so small and weighed like nothing. As, I walked towards the exit Gabriel called my name and I stopped in my tracks.

Gabriel walked towards me, worry written all over his face. His eyes roamed over Beth's still body in my arms and the hardness in his face softened. "Is she alright?"

"Just tired." I replied, sighing. "She used a lot of her energy during the session and she's too weak to walk back to her rooms."

"My stuff…"

I looked down to see her closed eyes and small hand grasping the front of my shirt. "My stuff is still in the locker room."

Gabriel nodded, seeming to understand, and called Kimberly over. She was standing next to us in a matter of seconds, her eyes filled with concerned as she looked at Beth. "Will you grab Beth's things out of her locker?"

"Sure." She said. Turning to Beth, she laid a hand on her forehead and muttered something underneath her breath. It sounded like a prayer for healing. "I'll bring them over to your room, sweetie."

Beth opened her eyes and smiled up at Kimberly. Her eyes tender with gratitude. "Thank you." She turned to me and muttered, "I don't know why you and Kim fight. Doesn't make sense."

My eyes grew wide and I looked up to see Kimberly's cheeks flushed and Gabriel's smirk. "I don't know either, Beth. I don't know either."

I could have punched him right then and there for further acknowledging Beth's statement. Kimberly blushed even further and idly played with her hands. She was uncomfortable and I saw her glancing towards the door. Using my peripheral vision, I saw that Lucas was standing by the door, waiting for her.

"Well, if we're done here – I'd like to get back to her room to rest."

Gabriel crossed his hands over his chest and said, "After you're done, I'd like to speak to you."

"I think the proper axiom would be for me to speak with you." I said seriously. Gabriel clenched his jaw as his eyes began to turn a cold green. "I meant," I cleared my throat and he stood still, waiting for me to continue. "There needs to be an apology said from me." I looked towards Kimberly and added, "To both of you."

"I see." Gabriel muttered. "Well, I think there will be time for that later. Go get the kid to bed, Cal." He patted my shoulder and I turned to leave with Kimberly walking beside me.

"What's with the change of heart?" She asked.

She just couldn't accept a simple apology. "So you're saying I have a heart?"

She laughed, "How did you – oh, that's right. You are a mind reader. Telepathic, for the more technical term."

"That's right."

"Hey! Does that mean you've been…"

"Mhm." I said, amused. She was getting worked up about this new development of hers. I actually found all this quite entertaining. I realized that I liked making Kimberly all hot and bothered. Oh, God. Did I actually just think that?

"How can you violate someone's thoughts!" She asked aghast. "That's just sick! I don't ever want to know that you have read my mind ever again, Montgomery. If I do, you will be in a world of hurt."

"So now you want to hurt me? Never considered you'd be into the kinky bondage stuff, but I'll try anything once."

"You are unbelievable." She huffed and turned on her heels. She walked right pass Lucas and he followed after her with a confused expression on his face. "What's wrong," I heard him say before the door closed.

"That wasn't very nice. But it was funny." Beth said giggling.

"I thought so too." I said walking towards the exit. "C'mon, let's get you to bed. Enough dawdling. I bet it's past your bed time."

She huffed. "It's just seven o'clock! I am not some five year old."

I chuckled. "Alright, alright."

It was funny how I could have a full conversation with Beth but I couldn't talk to Kimberly for five minutes without bantering with her. Kimberly just stirred something inside me. She made me want to be more…? I shook off the thoughts and continued towards Beth's corridor. But as my mind wouldn't have it I kept on thinking about what Lucas said about Kimberly. Did he like her? But the bigger question was: Did she like him?

CHAPTER 5

I t was hours after the training session that I had received a telepathic message from Calder, telling me to meet him on the verandah located in the east side of the castle. The sun was beginning to set, casting the hall with dim shadows as I walked through the winding corridors. Other Keepers were bustling about getting ready for dinner in the dining hall as it was mandatory for each and every one of us unless you had special privileges or if the person was feeling ill and told to rest by Dr. Corvaul (our council doctor), but that rarely happened. I suppose Beth would be on bed rest after today, but then at the same time, she looked fine when Calder and her left.

Was it only Calder who was blind to the chemistry that him and Kimberly shared? If a fifteen year old can figure it out then why couldn't he? He needs a bloody hit to the head, that's what he needs. I chuckled from the thought. Yes. That was exactly what he needed. Maybe then he would get his bearings straight and see what is right in front of him.

The idea of knocking Calder upside the head was pretty damn amusing. Maybe Kim would be the one to do it for me - since those two were always bantering. One of these days it would end up with her beating the crap out of him.

"That would certainly be the day." I chuckled.

"Huh?"

I snapped my head up and saw Jessie's bemused expression. She was standing a few feet from an open archway where the last of the sunlight was streaming through. "You okay, Gabe?"

"Yeah. I'm fine..." There was a sudden flicker of a light ebbing from the passage behind Jessie. I stepped forward, disregarding Jessie's calls of concern. It wasn't the last rays of sunlight that I was seeing but something different, something out of this world. I narrowed my eyes and could see the slightest trace of a figure outlined by the window; the light surrounding its frame. As I get closer, the light begins to glow and I'm utterly en-thralled by whatever it might be. It's like I'm bewitched, caught in its magical hand, forgetting about everything except for the light in front of me. Never in my life have I seen something so beautiful and peaceful.

"Gabriel?" Jessie called, momentarily breaking me out of the trance.

"Do you see it?" I asked Jessie, keeping my eyes on the unearthly light.

I hear her footsteps on the wooden floor – distant and frag-mented like if we were both in two different worlds. "See what?" She asks, walking besides me. "I don't see anything Gabriel."

"You don't see that light?" I asked perplexed. "Surely you see it! It's right there in front of-" As I said those words the light suddenly faded. I blinked twice and rubbed my eyes, only to leave the trace of black spots in my vision. I know for a fact

that it wasn't just the trick of the light. Something was here –
something had been here.

"Gabriel? You sure you're okay? Maybe we should call Dr.
Corvoul. Have you been treated for any recent demon wounds?
Maybe that's it. Or maybe you're exhausted. You have been
training hard over the past few days - not to mention that you
also had a recent mission."

"Jessie." I said. "I'm fine." That was a lie, of course. I wasn't
fine. I was...confused, out of breath, intrigued...

"You should get going." I heard myself say but it was distant,
emotionless. "You don't want to be late for dinner." Turning
my back to her, I began walking towards the east wing, but not
without Jessie's deliberate persistence.

"What about you?" She asked. I heaved out a long sigh,
closing my eyes for a moment. I now remember the exact reason
why Calder broke up with her. She would always question
every move he made, constantly breathing down his neck with
nowhere to run; kind of how she was acting with me at the
moment.

I didn't turn around to face her instead I just remained as I was
and said in a hard tone, "I have somewhere else to be." Without
another word escaping my mouth, I left Jessie's protests behind
as I walked towards the east wing. Whatever that light was I
needed to tell Calder about it immediately. I knew that there
was a perfectly good explanation for it, but at the moment I had
no idea what that cause could be.

"What do you think?" Gabriel asked, leaning over the railing.
He was looking out at the gardens where different various of
flowers grew. There were yellow peonies, violet lilies, vibrant

red roses, all kinds of flowers that gave the air, well, a flowery scent.

Gabriel had come into the verandah with a distressed look in his eyes. Before I could even ask what was wrong, he began to tell me what he saw in the corridor before coming here. There was something puzzling about the entire occurrence. The most puzzling was Gabriel's reaction. Why did he think that this was so important? "Don't know. I'm sure there is something about it on file or in books. Maybe check the records?"

He scoffed. "That could take weeks. Sometimes, I wish this place would upgrade to the twenty-first century. Have the entire collection of records on a database we could create…"

"Well, good luck with that. You know how they are. They like things to be exactly like in the medieval era. Surely, Rocovik was born then. He probably likes how things are now. Oh, wait, it's the same; nothing new."

He continued to look down at the garden, lost in his own thoughts. There was a wishful look in his eyes as he played idly with the chain around his neck. He was remembering and as much as I wanted to know what the memory was I decided not to take a peek into his thoughts. I was ready to make amends with Gabriel – that is why I called him here – but, things had taken on a new turn. Even without the apology, things between us had settled back to normal. That's how it was with us. There didn't need to be an apology said verbally – he just knew.

It still completely puzzled me why he would still think of her. I was sorry that I had said those things about her last night, but I didn't get it. She was just a mortal girl. They would come and go as the centuries passed us. He was completely delusional for loving her. Gwen had probably already forgotten about him. He was mentally decapitating himself for still holding on to whatever they had. It has been seven years for heaven's sakes…I think it's time to move on. He could never have a future with her, so what was the point of holding on to the past? There was no point. He needed to find a girl who was a Keeper - someone who would be there with him for all of eternity; whenever that ended.

There were lots of girls that would be a perfect match for him; girls that would surely love him in return if he'd only let go of Gwen.

"I heard your conversation with Kim earlier…what was that about?" He asked still looking over the railing.

I chuckled. Well this certainly was a change of topic. "You heard that?" He nodded and I saw the ghost of a smile playing on his lips. "Nothing really. Just some fun chit-chat."

"Uh-huh." He didn't believe me by the sound of his voice. He was grinning from ear to ear and I wanted to punch him to stop whatever mischievous thought he was about to utter. "Why don't you tell her you like her? It's blatantly obvious that you do."

And there was the thought. I scoffed. "Yeah, right. She's infuriating but quite fun to mess with because she gets all hot and bothered and her nose kinda scrunches up in-"

Shit. What the hell was the matter with me? "I didn't…" my mouth had become dry all of a sudden and I took a swig of my bottle of wine, only making my throat burn in the process. "I don't like her," I sputtered.

"You sure about that? You get really defensive whenever I bring her up. Care to tell me why that is?"

"Actually, no. Because I don't know." Heaving out a deep breath, I turned my attention to the garden below and froze. I felt my body tense up and before I knew it the bottle in my hand shattered into a million jagged pieces. "Shit."

"What the hell was that?"

I ducked underneath the railing and began to pick up the broken fragments from the ground, glancing down at the garden all the while. She was with Lucas walking down the winding paths, a light flickering from his hands. I heard the distant sound of laughter, light and cheery like morning sleigh bells on Christmas morning.

"Ahh...I see. And you say you don't like her." Gabriel kneeled down and helped me collect pieces of the broken glass in his hands. "It looks like you'll have some competition there, Cal."

"Yeah, right." I scoffed. "There's no competition if there is no game, Gabriel." I peeked through the railing and saw Lucas giving her a fire show. He was playing with small balls of fire, throwing each one in the air in turn while catching them as they fell. It was sort of like juggling, but normally jugglers don't play with fire or have more than two balls in the air. "Besides, Lucas is a great guy. Bet he'd make her happy."

"Don't you think you can make her happy?"

I looked up and met Gabriel's questioning gaze. He was serious even though his tone had been light, casual. But the question was more than that. It was like coming to a wall and not knowing what to do. The obvious answer would be to climb it or tear it down. Isn't that what I wanted? Did I really want to live my life without having anyone to share it with?

"No," I mumbled, "I don't think I can." Picking up the last of the glass, I stood up and heard her laughter echoing through my mind, giving me a sense of longing – wishing that I could be the one to make her laugh like that. I then heard the distant sound of Lucas' laugh cutting through my reverie, causing my body to tense again. Unconsciously, I must have gripped the pieces of glass in my hand too tightly because I heard Gabriel's bewildered voice saying, "What the hell are you doing? Are you out of your mind?" He gripped my shoulder and steered me away from the railing.

I looked at him, confused at his outburst and once we were away from the sights of the garden, I followed his gaze to my hands. I was bleeding, blood running down my hand, splattering on the marble floor. The ironic part of it was that I couldn't even feel it. The pain instead was in my chest; while Kimberly's beautiful bluish-green eyes filled my mind. Looking down at my palm I saw the wound healing before my eyes, slow and exact. I looked up to see Gabriel's brows strewn down in concern and confusion. I frowned, not saying anything more of the matter and walked out of the verandah, towards the shelter of my room where I wouldn't be bothered to explain, and that was the last thing I wanted.

Books were scattered all over the table I was using in the far corner of the library. Some were stacked on top of each other – unopened- while others were open but tossed to a corner because of their useless information. So far I had come up empty with my search of the light I saw earlier. There was nothing that indicated what it could possibly have been. My first thought was that it was a ghost. It was a far stretched theory. I'd never confronted a ghost, but I heard that they were real. This place was centuries old, and it was highly possible that a person's ghost could still linger and roam the castle walls.

But that wouldn't explain the light.

If it was a ghost it would certainly not be peaceful.

It wouldn't be beautiful.

Grabbing another book from my stack, I opened it to the index and skimmed through the subtitles finding nothing interesting or new. It was just a list of different kinds of demons. The next book I grabbed was about ghosts; useless, since I ruled out that possibility.

"Why must this be so difficult?" I said aloud. There was no one beside me in the library. Looking up at the clock, I read that it was half past midnight. "Great. Hours of slaving over these books and I have nothing to gain for it." Sighing in resignation, I started to collect some books to put back in their rightful shelves. There must have been about fifty of them cluttering the desk, and I felt bad leaving them for Gretchen to pick up and clean after me. I would leave some for her to put away, but certainly not all of them.

I couldn't get over what had happened earlier today. It was strange yet oddly beautiful and captivating. I know for a fact that it wasn't a figment of my imagination. Maybe, it was a new power I was developing...? Hmm...but that didn't quite make sense. For one, we develop all our gifts within the year we find out we are "special". I first started to develop my heightened senses while I was still living in Fairfield. It was strange at first because I didn't know what was going on. I thought that my hearing was improving and my eye sight becoming sharp and exact, noting the smallest of details. It wasn't until one afternoon where Gwen and I were in town hanging out with friends that everything changed.

It was just another normal day out with friends. We were walking along the sidewalk and about to cross the street when Gwen stopped to tie her shoe before continuing forward. I was running behind because I saw a new skateboard on one of the shop windows and went in to ask the price. It was too much as I should have known, but I just had to ask anyway. I quickly caught up to my friends and was only a few steps behind when Gwen stopped for a few seconds to tie her shoe and resumed to cross the street all in the duration of a minute.

On her first step to cross the street – at the same time- I heard a series of panicking screams. It was like everything was in slow motion. I saw Gwen in front of me, walking slowly towards the other end of the sidewalk and then I saw the woman in her car; a small boy was sitting the passenger seat also screaming and crying. She wasn't stopping and I realized that her brakes were out. Without giving it another thought, I ran forward and pulled Gwen back.

It was just at the right moment because the next second time resumed to normal and the car whizzed by, crashing into the park gate across the street. Everything came back into focus as the cacophony of sounds exploded in my eardrums. It was unbearable, but having Gwen in my arms somehow made it tolerable. I focused all my attention on her and held her, murmuring that it was all okay. Gwen was in hysterics, clinging to me saying over and over again, "oh my god". She was in shock at realizing that her life could have been over just a few moments before.

After that, came the questions. First from the police – they wanted to know the specifics and details of the accident. Then from my parents, and I told them of the event. As I explained the feeling of time slowing down, both of my parents smiled (which I found odd) and then frowned. It was that day that they explained what I was – what we were – and began the preparations to leave. They told me that we couldn't stay here any longer now that I had come into my gifts. We had to leave and go to the Council in Italy where my father could resume the position of Head Council and I could begin my training.

It was overwhelming.

Part of me wanted to go and train – it all sounded so fascinating and remarkable. But the other part of me wanted to stay because of Gwen. I couldn't bear to leave her behind after so many years of being friends. She was the only person who knew every single thing about me. I couldn't get away with anything because she'd know I was hiding something or lying. The last few months were difficult, but she never guessed it. She never guessed what I was or that I was keeping the biggest secret of my life. Gwen never found out the truth for the best, but it kills me every day.

I regret not saying goodbye to her. She deserved that much but I had no choice in the matter. If only I could see how she is, maybe then I could let it go, but I'm not even allowed that chance. There aren't words to describe how much she meant to me. No one understands – not even Calder. He doesn't even understand his own feelings so how would he even comprehend mine?

Sighing, I walked out of the library and into the corridor's vast darkness. Saying a quick spell I lighted the torches that ran along the walls, one by one as I walked pass they burst to life – illuminating the hall with a dim amber glow. It wasn't until I got to the end of the hall that I saw the same unearthly glow by one of the windows. It wasn't the light from the flames or the moonlight – I was certain. This was a whole different kind of light. It was almost like a golden color, warm and beautiful.

My steps became cautious as I came closer to it, and for some reason I said, "Don't be afraid. I won't hurt you." The light seemed to understand and stayed in place until I was a few inches in front of it. Then, it vanished like before. One second it was there and then the next it wasn't. But this time it was different. I noticed something that I had not seen earlier: A corner of white flowing fabric and the outline of a hand.

Maybe, it was a ghost.

CHAPTER 6

Training sessions commenced, which meant that Beth and I spent most of the afternoon together developing her telekinesis. Unfortunately, that also meant that Kimberly and Lucas were spending more time together and – not to mention – growing closer. It was something that I did not enjoy seeing, and something that Gabriel noticed even when I tried to mask the emotions that were unreadable to everyone but him.

As the weeks went by, Beth began to get a grip on her gift. She had come a long way from our first training session together; from being unable to lift a simple book to her lifting something that weighed more than fifty pounds using her mind. It was extraordinary! It was quite an improvement and I was extremely proud of the kid. I also observed Kimberly from across the training room and saw that she had also improved from her first day of training with Lucas. After the plate incident there wasn't anything else shattered, well maybe except my...

I shook my head to clear my mind and looked at Beth levitating a fifty pound weight. She was standing up, raising her hand as the weight lifted effortlessly in the air. The kid wasn't even breaking a sweat, and it showed how far she'd come since the first day when she nearly fainted because of all the magic she had used. I vowed that I wouldn't let her use magic to that extent again, and we worked from there - each day using a little more until she was using her full power, and was okay physically and mentally. My method worked and slowly she began to build her strength in her magic and was able to slowly progress with her telekinesis. By the end of her training she will be able to lift anything twice her weight. Hell, maybe even quadruple her weight like a truck or a marble statue. It would definitely come in handy in battle if she loses her weapon. Beth could easily just plunge it into the demon and kill it without working too hard physically.

"Alright, everyone." Gabriel said, calling us all to attention. Each group stopped working and turned to face him. Their faces were a mix of wonder and awe as their eyes settled on Gabe. The awe feeling was mostly seen in the girls since they all had some sort of crush on him. They all respected him and thought he was 'so dreamy and broken it's mysterious.' Broken, yes. Mysterious? I don't know what to say about that one. Dreamy? Ha. Not even going to go there.

But all of them knew that Gabriel didn't date, which made him all the more attractive in their eyes. I will never understand the mind of a teenage girl. You'd think that they'd accept that fact, but no they had hope that whatever he was going through will one day disappear. Thus, falling in love with one of them, and having a happily ever after; riding off into the eternal sunset.

Yeah, right. If such a thing ever existed.

"I'm very proud to see each and every one of you improving in your powers." I caught Gabriel saying. Zoning out was beginning to be a serious problem for me. Focusing, I paid my attention to what he was saying. "You have definitely come a long way these past two months. The strength, determination, and dedication you all have shown have definitely opened up my eyes to the potential each of you have in the future. I believe that you all will be great Keepers and I know it's too soon to make that assumption, but I've never seen a group quite like this one. Give yourselves a hand for accomplishing your first five months of training."

Gabriel clapped and everyone joined in with smiles and hugs accompanying their partners. Beth looked at me timidly and I opened my arms for her to embrace me. She smiled and ran forward, crushing her body to mine in a warm embrace. I was caught off guard by the open affection that she showed towards me. It was something new that I'd never experienced. She was so little and adorable that I couldn't help but like the kid like a sister. Heaven knows that she acted like one.

"Thank you, Cal! You are the best teacher ever!"

"Obviously," I said laughing and she joined in with me. "No, but seriously. You are a very good student, which made it easier for me to teach you. I agree with Gabriel. You have what it takes to be a Keeper and more potential than you know. Remember that." She pulled back and smiled at me making her dimples show on each cheek and lighting up her brown eyes.

"Thank you so much, Cal." She whispered into my t-shirt before pulling back and turning around to wipe her eyes with her sleeve.

"Beth, are yo-"

"With that being said," Gabriel continued after the applause and celebration died down. I couldn't ask Beth what was wrong so instead I put my arm around her shoulder and pulled her close to me. She smiled up at, her eyes glassy with gratitude.

"I will be giving all of you a week off." Did I hear right? He was cancelling training for a week? Cheers of joy erupted from the novices, each jumping up with glee and murmurs of shopping and long leisure weekdays out with friends filled the room. Well, their reaction certainly answered my question. "Enjoy it. Everyone have a good week. Class is dismissed."

Everyone started to pack until Gabriel called the Keepers to him – that was me and the others who helped with the training sessions. There wasn't a word for us since we weren't fully Keepers yet, but calling us transitionals would just sound odd. Better to just call us Keepers since that is what we become when we turn twenty-two and complete the rite of passage.

When the nine of us gathered around Gabe he began his spiel. "Great work everyone. It truly is good to see you helping out with the novices and each of you developing your own relation-ship with your partner. Some were already there but others were new, and I was glad to see that you didn't ostracized them after training was over." There was a few scoffs from Trenton and Aiden. Gabriel gave them a hard stare and they quickly quieted down. I crossed my arms over my chest, rolling my eyes at their completely immature selves.

"I know that that isn't what is normally done, but I asked each of you to come and help Cal and I in this class because we thought it was a good idea." He said. But that wasn't entirely true. It had been his idea and I might have agreed if I hadn't been an arrogant ass the night before. "It turned out we were right and I concur this a success. Wouldn't you agree?"

Anna, Lily, and Stacey all nodded their heads in agreement and smiled at Gabriel. Well it was more of a flirty smile considering the twists they did to their hair as they looked at him. Gabe was completely oblivious and it amazed me how blind he could be. Jessie just nodded and glared at me. Well, I guess she still had sore feelings. It's been months for heaven's sakes. The girl needed to get over the fact of our breakup.

Nole and Lucas smiled and agreed with the idea. Well, I know why Lucas was smiling. It was his chance to spend time with Kimberly – to get to know her for who she is. Clenching my jaw, I waited impatiently for Gabriel to dismiss us. If this was all that he had to say he could have said it to us earlier or he could have told me how good of a job I was doing.

"Cal, you have anything to add?"

Furrowing my eyebrows, I looked at him questioningly and then remembered where I was. Right, needed to add something. "I think you touched on all of it. I know some of us are happier about working with the novices than others," I pointedly looked at Lucas, directing my comment towards him. His posture stiffened as he crossed his hands over his chest. "Just remember to keep it at a professional level."

Lucas starred at me with obvious anger in his eyes. He was astonished at my remark, but mostly seething with loathing as I read his mind. A series of curses were being said through the walls of his brain; none being verbally said. He didn't have the guts to start something in front of everyone else. I felt the hard and unbelievable stares from our circle, but I couldn't care less. When did Calder Montgomery care about what other's thought? Gabriel cleared his throat and gave me a hard look. "Well," he stared, obviously at a loss for words by the way that his eyes shifted from mine to Lucas. "That's it everyone. Enjoy your week off and be ready bright an early the week after."

As everyone began to take their leave, Gabriel clasped his hand around my shoulder. "What was that?" He asked, curiosity mixed with annoyance filling his voice. "Couldn't you have handled your personal endeavors outside of the room? If Kim and Lucas' relationship is bothering you so much than maybe you should tell her how you feel, you idiot."

"I'm an idiot? You're the-" I completely caught off where that thought was going. I did not need him to be angry with me again. "You're the one who encourages their relationship," I said instead. "I thought you were my friend. You're supposed to have my back."

He sighed, "Cal," he ran a hand through his hair; an obvious sign of resignation. "Look, I know it's hard for you to express your feelings, but if you really like Kim you should tell her. Don't let her get away from you, if that is what you want. Because right now it looks like you are fighting a battle within. You need to figure out what you want before you go looking for trouble."

"Trouble is my middle name." I said, ignoring his advice.

He shook his head. "You've got a lot to learn," was all he said before he disappeared right before my eyes leaving me dumbfounded and irate.

"Damn. Lucky bastard and his magic." I muttered. "What is that supposed to mean?"

Walking the gardens with the overcast sky above me, I pondered what exactly I wanted. After spending almost an hour roaming the winding paths – I still didn't have an answer. It wasn't something that I had ever asked myself. What did I want? I had everything I wanted or...did I? Gabriel's piece of advice didn't leave me with an answer, but instead with more questions than I had ever wished for.

I don't know what came over me after training was over. Was it Lucas who I was angry with or was it Kimberly? Could it be jealously what I had been feeling at that moment? Seeing them together just stirred something inside of me. There was this unknown feeling at the core of my stomach whenever I saw them together. The way that she was so carefree with him and the way he looked at her made me want to turn away or punch him right in the face. But, why the animosity? Why did I want to hurt him? Why was I feeling like something was burning inside of me? What did I want?

"Ugh!" I kicked a pebble in my path and it hit one of the small white gazebos that were placed around the garden. There were at least five alone on this side of the castle, each different from the last with its intricate architecture and foundation. It amazed me how well intact my home was after years of its development.

The castle alone must have been erected in the sixteenth century. It must have been quite an interesting time in our history, since it was in the middle of the Renaissance Age. It was a new cultural movement in that time; involving literature, art, science, and politics. The castle itself was built with that era in mind. Imagine the Chateau de Chambord composted with a central keep with four immense bastion towers at the corners.

The keep forming part of the front wall of a larger compound with two more large towers placed in the middle as our main building. Then there was the elaborately developed roof line that looked like the skyline of a town. There were different types of chimneys, bell towers, and winding double staircases leading up to an empty, desolate tower. Its white granite stones making it look more like a castle from a fairytale rather than a home for supernatural beings. Inside, the soaring semicircular archways that are displayed in the entries of each corridor were a wonder all on their own.

Then there was the extensive gardens that surrounded the castle with water features like a beautiful fountain with statues by the great Michealangelo himself in the north wing, a waterfront that overlooked the never ending forestry that ran on that side.

The people in the town called this place Castello di Tempo - Castle of Time. It was rumored to by the castle that has withstood time itself, and that it has been owned by the same family for centuries; never being on the market for sale. There were so many stories surrounding the castle, but none could come close to the inhabitants of the place, my home.

As I kept on walking forwards, I noticed that there was someone sitting in the gazebo that I'd hit with the rock. Getting closer I noticed that it was Kimberly sitting quietly on the rocking settee as she looked out onto the garden lost in her thoughts. Her place there in the vast gazebo made her small in frame. It was like she painted out of a story book; a lonely girl with the clouds grey above her head and the lively greenery of the plants around her, making it all a painting come to life before my eyes.

She was wearing regular blue jeans and a light dark purple sweater that made her hair look lighter that it really was, and also gave her the appearance that she was in the present rather than in some painting caught in its shoot for all of eternity. She must have known that I was watching because her back became rigid as she turned around and glanced at me, turning her attention back to the beautiful scene in front of her. It was only a glance but that glance said it all. It was the kind of glance that could freeze you in place because of the weight the look held. She didn't want me here, I knew as I read the thoughts running through her head about me.

Thoughts like: What is he doing here? Why can't I seem to escape him? Ugh. Is he just here to yell at me because if so I'm so leaving. Why is he still standing there? I can feel him staring at me. Why is he staring at me? What does he want?

"Why are you here all alone?" I asked after a few moments of awkward silence. She didn't turn back to look at me and I found it quite rude, and a form of bad manners. Did she even know where her place was especially since she was a novice. Just because she was the same didn't mean that she could disrespect her superiors – meaning me.

Great, question genius, she thought.

I took that to offense. Here I am trying to be nice and she had to be sarcastic and rude! Well, she didn't know that I had read the verbal response to my question, and seeing that she wasn't looking at me, she didn't see my reaction.

"Looking for some peace and quiet but that's ended now." She turned back around to look at me and something changed in her expression. Was it something that she saw in my face? I was utterly at a loss for words as I leaned back on the archway of the gazebo. Her face softened and she asked, "Why are you here?"

"Now, that is a particularly good question." I said, fending for light amusement. It worked because she gave me a small smile that causes her eyes to sparkle a lush evergreen like the trees that surrounded the property. "Just taking a leisure stroll around the gardens, thinking about nothing about everything."

"Seems to be the thing you like to do most."

"What do you mean?" I was suddenly very curious. Kimberly beckoned me to come and sit beside her on the settee and I did as she wanted. She scooted over to make room for me and I was suddenly very cautious of how close our bodies were. There were only a few inches separating us from touching. Looking down, I saw how she brought up one of her legs and put her arms around it, resting her chin on her knee.

"You're always so absorbed in your thoughts. Either from listening to other's minds or being caught up in yours. I wonder sometimes what you could possibly be thinking that makes the whole world disappear. Or maybe you take time to come up with your extremely arrogant remarks." She turned her head towards me and smiled as I did the same. "You know, you are quite a puzzle to solve. Not a very easy task."

"Where's the fun where everyone knows who you are? I think it's quite amusing."

"So you like people to think you are someone else rather than who you really are?"

"No, that's not what I meant. Why should people know everything about me? Isn't it my choice to let them in?"

"That's the problem," she muttered. "You don't let anyone in." Kimberly sighed and stood up, idly fidgeting with her scarf as she headed out of the gazebo. She was looking down at the ground as she slowly walked down the stairs and into the garden's winding paths. I didn't know what to say to her statement. What could she possibly have meant with those words?

"Wait up!" I called, jumping out of my seat and running towards the direction I saw her go. I need to know what she meant but chasing after someone was all new to me that I didn't know what to even feel. The only thing I chased was demons and that was to kill them. Kimberly was an entirely different manner. Her expression had been so somber that I wondered why the statement had made her sad. I run after her and after a few minutes I find that I'm being lead into a wild goose chase. She was playing games with me now – the only objective I had was to find her now.

I heard a fit of giggles to the left of me and quickly darted in that direction, but I didn't see her. There were hundreds of flowers plotted on the ground that it was the perfect place to hide behind the brushes. I must have looked like a complete madman searching for her in this endless land of flowers and thorns. Being momentarily distracted with her enthralling laughter, I walked into a bed of roses and pricked my skin. It hurt like hell, but the scratches immediately healed making the pain last only for a split second.

I was definitely going to get some pay back after I found her. Why was I even continuing this game of charades? I'd stop right now and walk back to the castle and have some lunch. I think they were serving fettuccini alfredo for dinner, my favorite.

Maybe even have a nice bottle of red wine to accompany my dinner. Wine makes everything better. It really was a shame that we couldn't get drunk.

"Hey, Cal!" I turned around to see Kimberly running forward and jumping on me, making me fall hard on my back with Kimberly sprawled on top of me. "Ha! Got you for once. How does it feel to be caught off guard?"

"What the hell are yo-?" I asked but quickly clasped my mouth shut. Her face was mere inches away from mine. Her lips delicate, smooth and a soft glossy pink that smelled vaguely of watermelon. I reach forward with my hand to smooth back the strand of hair that fell on her face, but stopped. It was all disorienting, feeling the light huff of her breath on my skin. "You have-don't you have a boyfriend?" I uttered getting my bearings straight. Thinking about Lucas made my blood boil hot and made me come back to reality. "I don't think he'd be too happy if we were caught in this position."

Kimberly's eyes widened and she pushed me back as she got up from on top of me. "What are you talking about?" She brushed the invisible dirt from her jacket, and I saw that it was all a diversion to hide the blush that splayed on her face.

"Lucas." I said his name with more scorn than I had wished. "I know you two are an item and I wouldn't want to be caught in a bloody crossfire with him. That guy could probably send me to smithereens - not that he'll ever get the chance, of course. No doubt he'd want to burn me to a bloody pulp if he finds out about this."

She scoffed. "What? You thought that this was something?" There was no softness in either her voice or eyes; the moment in the gazebo long forgotten. "This was nothing, if you can manage to get that through your thick skull."

"Really?" I stride forward and stand inches in front of her. Her breath catches and I smirk seeing the vulnerability that the mere space causes. Leaning to whisper in her ear I say, "Could have fooled me by the way you threw yourself at me. Very original. Never had that done before."

She backed away, obvious hurt in her eyes as she took several steps back until she was far from me. "Stay away from me and stay out of my business you arrogant jerk. Just when I think you are an actual human being you turn into an ass."

"C'mon. What does a guy have to do to get some fun around here?"

"How about being nice once in awhile!" She called back as she walked towards the side entrance of the east wing.

Be nice? Ironically enough that was the same thing that Gabriel had said to me a couple of months back. Wasn't I being nice beforehand? I honestly don't know what she stirred inside of me. One moment everything is fine and going smoothly and the next she is walking away, infuriated; leaving me utterly at a loss for words every single time.

I scoffed, walking back inside to have a heaping plate of fettuccine and alfredo with wine. That should make everything better and have this scene long forgotten. After all, alcohol certainly makes everything better in my book.

CHAPTER 7

Having a week of was certainly not something I was accustomed to ever since I can remember. I had no recollection of ever getting a break since I was fourteen. It was unheard of and I didn't exactly know how to feel about the whole thing. Ironically enough, it was exactly the unexpected turn of how my life was becoming.

What was a guy to do for a whole week without having to train?

"Paris."

"Paris?" I asked puzzled. What the hell were we going to do in Paris?

"A bunch of us are taking a trip down there. Should be fun. Thought you'd want to go." Gabriel said, grabbing an empty suitcase and starting to pack. He aimlessly grabbed shirts and jeans from his wardrobe and tossed it into his suitcase.

"Who's going?" I asked, taking a seat on his desk chair and propping my feet up on the desk. "Anyone that I could be seen associating with?"

He scoffed. "Don't you mean people who would want to associate with you?"

"Ha. Ha. Funny. I mean it. Who's all going?"

Gabriel stopped packing and cocked his left eyebrow, his scar visibly showing in the light. It would forever be a remembrance of the night when the Kelifeo demon subdued him. "Don't you mean to ask if she's going?"

"Will you stop answering my questions with questions!" Exasperated, I grabbed one of the paperweights on his desk and threw it at him. He caught it before it hit him – not that I thought that anything more was going to happen.

"Will you relax? I'm just messing with you. What is with you? You seem more peeved than usual."

I gritted my teeth, annoyed that he could read me so damn well. That's what I got for having a best friend. Did all best friends know the other so well like Gabriel and I? I wondered about that. Many of us kept to ourselves before we went through the rite of passage to become a full pledged Keeper because of the danger being a transitional brought on our lives. Once you were highly trained you were sent on missions to prove yourself. If we returned after our first one than it meant there was a higher chance of surviving the next one after that. The system also was set to separate the weak from the strong. The Council did not want Keepers who will be defenseless and powerless against evil. Thus, the ones who died are nothing more than casualties for those who do survive. What are a couple of hundred lives against thousands of us who survive, and fight evil for centuries?

It was different for me and Gabriel, though. Ever since we were teenagers, it was certain that we would both survive by the skill we demonstrated from the very start. Our determination, agility, strength, and wisdom at that age excelled most of our age group. Looking back, I can see why we were chosen for many of the missions that we were assigned to, and it's because we would get the job done and return safely home afterwards.

But there was always the question and the fear of not coming back home; it was always probable. Not likely, but possible. Could that be the reason why I shut people out as Kimberly insinuated? After thinking a while about her words in the gazebo it was the only conclusion I could muster. It was also the only logical one.

"So you coming or not?" Gabriel asked. I looked up to see his suit case packed and ready to go, the latch barely keeping it shut.

"Wait, what? Now? Since when did you finish?" Blinking, I saw the last beams of sunlight streaming in through the window. Where had all the time gone?

"Yes, Cal. Are you alright? You look a bit perplexed – kind of disoriented. Maybe, you shouldn't go. You can always stay and manage the castle with the staff."

"What are you? A comedian?" Standing up from my seat, I headed for the door and stopped dead in my tracks. There was something bright reflecting from the corner of his wardrobe mirror. "What is that?" I turn around and see that a small orb is floating near the window. Gabriel turns his head, his body freezing at the sight of the object.

"It's her again." He breathes out in awe. "I didn't think I'd see her again."

As soon as he said those words, the light disappeared as if nothing was ever there in the first place. The room dims to its normal lighting, leaving the warmth and glow that the light had provided. I shiver as cold air travels down my back. "What on earth are you talking about, Gabe?"

He turns back around to face me, his eyes wide but full of awed and happiness…? "Gabriel, what was that?"

"It was the light I told you about. I never told you, did I?"

"Yes, you did. Remember? We were up on the verandah. It was the same day I hurt my hand."

"No," He shook his head and slumped down on the bed, his head in his hands. "I mean yes, I remember. But I didn't tell you that I saw her again."

I stared at him in complete confusion until he starts to tell me about his run in with his ghost later that same night. His whole body sacks in resignation, but also in something that I've never seen before: peace. His face loses all trace of sadness and becomes animated with light and joy. It's strange yet oddly welcoming. He speaks about the ghost as if it was someone who is lost and needed his help. He feels important that it is coming to him, and was glad that it had appeared to him again.

"Somehow she needs me to help her or cross her over. Or maybe she just wants a companion. I don't know, but I feel this sense of peace when she appears like she knows I need it, and she's trying to comfort me."

"Gabriel." I said, my voice sounding hard even to my own ears. I needed to bring him back to reality even if my words would hurt him. "What makes you think it's a ghost? Ghosts don't carry peace with them. On the contrary, they are tormented over the fact that they are dead and haven't crossed over. What makes you think that whatever we just saw is a ghost? It goes against every myth and legend we hear about."

"How do you know? Have you ever seen a ghost?"

I shook my head. "Then don't start demeaning my theory. It's possible and until it's proven otherwise I am going to believe that it is what it is; a ghost."

"Okay, okay." I said, holding my hands up surrender. I wasn't going to get anywhere when his mind was dead set on something. "Whatever you say, this is your problem. I won't meddle."

"Good." He sighed, standing up and taking his luggage in tow. "So, you coming or not?"

"I'll meet you at the front gates in half an hour. How are we getting there? Train or flying?"

"No. How else would we get there?" I furrowed my brow and he chuckled at my bemused expression. I stared blankly at him until he said, "Magic."

Of course.

"Welcome, young Italy Keepers," The head council elder of the French Council's voice echoes in the chamber. I look around me at the others and see how nervous they are by standing in front of the council. Looking at Kimberly, I see her standing up straight and erect, giving off the look of a poised Keeper rather than an anxious novice.

" We are all pleased that you are here for your vacation. I hear that the young Montehue and Montgomery have been training the novices diligently." Elder Dupont continued, looking at

Gabriel and me with a satisfied smile. "We have prepared each of your living quarters in the north side of the castle.

Since there are many of you, each room has been furnished for three people. Mr. Castnoff," a man not much older than me stepped forward and bowed his head in greeting as we all did the same. "He shall show you to your rooms. Please, enjoy your stay here and don't hesitate to ask if any of you need any assistance."

Gabriel and I stepped forward, bowing our heads in gratitude to the French Council. "Thank you for allowing our group to frequent our stay. I know that it was short notice-"

Dupont cleared his throat, stopping Gabriel from further continuing. "How can I deny Elder Montehue's son and friends?" He gave a raspy laugh, hinting at how old he was. He looked to be around seventy, but he must be more than five hundred centuries old.

We aged differently than humans. We were in a sense immortal, aging a year every fifty years. When a century passed our physical body would have only grown to be two years older. Many of us reached to be as old as or possibly even older than Dupont, but of course not all of us did.

"If there is nothing more...you are all excused. Accept my apologies for the haste, but there are matters we need to attend to." Dupont said, glancing at his co-council. Everyone else understood that it was council business and began to make their way towards the exit where Castnoff waited.

There was something extremely wrong with the way that Dupont said those words. Like if there really was a grave matter that needed immediate attention. Departing from the group, I turn around and walk forward to stand before the council. "I'd like to offer my services if you need them, sir. I know that it isn't my place, but if you need me I'll be honored to do so."

Hearing footsteps behind me, I see Gabriel approaching as the others are ushered out of the chamber. He stands beside me saying, "I would also like to offer my services in any way that I can, sir."

Dupont's chair scrapped against the wooden floor as he slowly rose to his feet, but as he did his knee gives out on him and he stumbles before being caught by one of the other members beside him. "Thank you, Levil'o. I'm not as young as I use to be, eh?" Levil'o gave him a tight smile as worry creased his brow. "It will be time for me to retire soon, but not today gentlemen."

Looking back at both me and Gabriel, Dupont said, "I have heard many stories about both of you and I have to say that I believe in what they say." There was a small smile on his mouth and the look of admiration in his eyes like how a grandfather would be proud of his grandchildren when they make something out of scratch. Like a ceramic cup or drawing. "You two are noble, honorable, and deadly. There is no doubt in my mind that you could help here, but this is a matter for our own to handle. We greatly appreciate and acknowledge your valor and dedication to serve, but I would not want to send you on a mission without your council's approval, and I would not even do so if they did approve. I'm afraid that this is a matter for full pledged Keepers."

"We understand." Gabriel and I said simultaneously as we bowed our head to leave. "Our offer still stands if you decide otherwise, sir." I added.

"I will keep that in mind, Mr. Montgomery."

Taking our exit, we stepped out of the chamber and followed the sound of voices down the torch lit corridor until we caught up to our group. Darkness had descended as we made our way to our living quarters, our footsteps echoing on the cobblestones. This castle was much older than ours was judging by the inadequate ventilation and flooring system. At least, our home had had the means to renovate without destroying the castle's architecture. It looked like they hadn't done any renovations. God, I really hope they have indoor plumbing.

We took up the rear, which gave us time to talk about what occurred inside the council's chambers; allowing us some semblance of privacy.

"What do you think?" I asked.

He shook his head, obviously perplexed as he ran his hand through his hair. "I don't know. I understand why he wouldn't send us since we aren't part of his council, but why he would say that the matter was only for pledge Keepers...? That part doesn't make sense."

"I agree. Do you think something is going on? Maybe, it's something we don't have the privilege of knowing yet. I hear that we aren't privy to all of the Council's secrets until we are fully pledged Keepers."

"Maybe..."

I shrugged. "Like he said, it's their problem to handle. We shouldn't dwell on it. Did you say we were here to have fun and not go on mundane missions?"

"Mundane? I didn't think that word would be in your vocabulary." He smirked, putting his arm around my shoulder. "But your right. We are here as a break for all the training and missions. Maybe, get Kimberly and you together. That will be my sole mission in life," he chuckled. "Well, for the week."

"Well, good luck with that." I said, looking at Kimberly in front of me. She was walking beside Lucas and seeing them caused the all too familiar heat course through my body. I jerked my head in their direction and Gabriel watched them as Lucas leaned in to whisper something in her ear. I gritted my teeth together and felt Gabriel's hand clasp my shoulder.

"They are just friends." He said.

I scoffed. "Could have fooled me...don't you see how close they are?"

Gabriel raised his eyebrow as a grin started forming at the corner of his mouth. "You really like her, don't you?"

Choosing to ignore his question I asked one of my own, "So who is going to be our second roommate?"

"What?" He asked looking at me incredulously. I shrugged not caring that I had changed the subject. Gabriel let it slide and thought for a moment before saying, "Lucas."

"What?" Now it was my turn to look at him disbelievingly. "You're joking. I am not rooming with him."

"Stop being such a girl. It might offer a chance to get to know what is going on with him and Kim. I know you want to know." He nudged me with his elbow and I rolled my eyes.

"Are you ever going to let it go?"

"Nope. Not until you admit your feelings for her. Then, maybe, I'll stop. It's quite amusing actually. No wonder you get a kick out of this sort of thing."

"Ha. Ha. I think you should quit this business and become a clown in the circus. But then again, you'd probably have tomatoes thrown at you for your lousy jokes."

He chuckled loudly, catching a few of the others attention – one of them being Kimberly. I caught her gaze for only a second before she narrowed her eyes at me with obvious annoyance and turned back around.

"So what do you say, Cal? Cal....Cal..."

"What?" I snapped. Gabe's amused expression shifted into one of concern and I mentally slap myself for taking my anger out on him. "Sorry...what were you saying?"

"Just about Lucas. But on second thought, I think I'll ask Nole. Less animosity in the room since I don't think putting the two of you in the same room will do any good."

"What is that supposed to mean? You don't think I can handle myself?"

"That's exactly what I'm saying. I'm glad that you understand." He said jokingly.

Rolling my eyes, I looked forwards and catch Kimberly's gaze once again as she turned back to look at us. I waved but she her lips part in surprise and quickly narrows her eyes, sending me dagger. The phrase 'if looks could kill' went through my mind. If the way she looked at me could kill me then I would have been dead a long time ago. No demon could paralyze me the way that she does, and the sad part was that she didn't even know.

She could never know. That would be like opening Pandora's Box; unleashing things that should be kept hidden and locked away.

CHAPTER 8

Gabriel didn't only have one sole mission for this trip. He had two. He was a benevolent dictator when it came to gathering us all up the next morning – like sheep, while he was our shepherd - for our Paris outing of the day. He even had an itinerary that he had worked on the night before. Who does that? Oh, that's right. Him.

Being here I thought that we would all go our separate ways and explore the city on our own with whomever we wanted, but that was not the case here. Sure, some of the Keepers and their novices went off on their own after getting Gabe's approval. What I found even more comical was that they actually asked him! I would have thought they'd just go off without him know-ing and have to answer to him later, but no – they actually asked. He had more respect from them than I thought. It was more than I could say for myself.

By the end of the morning there were only six of us left out of our group of nineteen. There was Beth who was idly snapping candid shots of us with her camera. She had already caught me in a not so attractive pose. I also saw her snap a photo of

Kimberly and Lucas; a smile on both of their faces as if there was nowhere else they'd rather be. Nole was quiet – keeping to himself as he walked besides Beth. His eyes roamed to his surroundings and finally settled on Beth, a smile forming on his lips as she took a picture of a couple ahead of us. She sighed dreamily and trotted on, snapping pictures of anything and everything. We were merely a canvas to her artistic eye as she found beauty all around her, even if I couldn't understand it.

Walking along the banks of the Seine River we came across many of the bridges that had been erected around the 1700's. There was so much history laid into the stones we walked under, each having their own story and place on record. Our group stopped on the Pont de la Concorde Bridge and we looked out at the city before us. On one side of the bridge I saw the faraway landmark that Paris was widely known for, the Eiffel Tower. The overcast sky made the Eiffel Tower look farther than it actually was, covering it with a light mist as the clouds rolled in from the North.

Looking down the Seine River, I saw decorative lights hanging casually along the bridge. They were golden brown with vines twining in the center of each light. Christmas was approaching and I counted in my head how far away it was until the festivities arrived. If I was correct it was only three weeks away as this was the first week of the month. It amazed me how easily I lost track of time when my sole purpose in life was protecting time from evil.

"Ha! Got you!" I heard Beth squeal as Gabriel stepped forward and seized her hand playfully.

"You got me unprepared! Aren't you supposed to tell us to say cheese before you take a picture?" He asked in mock outraged. I laughed at how carefree this day has been for all of us.

"Nope." She said popping the 'p'. "That's why they are called candid shots. I'm making something and it has to be as real as possible. No fake smiles or fake poses. Natural."

"But you didn't do that to Kimberly and Lucas." Gabriel said, crossing his hands over his chest. "I don't think it's fair at all."

"Hey," Kimberly said, smiling. "Don't bring us into this. Maybe, you should have been more guarded like we were." Looking at her I caught her eye and offered a small smile, but she quickly averted her eyes.

It had been like that all morning, and I had no idea what I had done to have vexed her so. Every time I'd catch her gaze she'd quickly avert her eyes or pull on a blank stare and turn her attention to Lucas, which he openly accepted. It angered me how she was acting towards me, and I didn't know why. I wasn't the kind to worry about what people thought. So why did I care about what she thought of me?

"Fine." I heard Gabriel say. His mouth was set in a straight line before it slowly turned into a smile that reached his eyes. He winked at Beth and she squealed once again, running off ahead of us where she took more pictures of bystanders with Nole a few feet behind her, an amused expression playing on his face.

We continued like this for the remainder of the morning until we headed back to the castle to get dressed for dinner. Gabriel had made reservations at this place called Café Moderne. It supposedly was a pretty lucrative and snazzy restaurant where formal attire was required. I opted for a black t-shirt and gray white stripped tweed jacket with gray slacks. I hadn't even realized that I'd packed 'formal' attire until I started rummaging through my suitcase.

Stepping back into the room I found Gabriel and Nole all dressed formally and ready to go. Gabriel wore a blue white stripped button up collared shirt with a navy blue – almost black – tie and khaki slacks. Nole chose to wear a white v-neck shirt with a light gray dinner jacket and regular black slacks. I was feeling a bit underdressed with my choice of clothing and almost turned to change into something more fitting, when there was a knock on the door.

Nole lazily walked towards the door to answer to a beautiful and elegant dressed Beth. Nole straightened his slack form and I heard a sudden intake of breath coming from both of them. Beth stared back at him with a starry gaze in her eyes for what seemed like hours, but in reality it was nothing more than mere seconds. Breaking the connection, she shook her head and looked down at her feet to hide the slight blush tinting her cheeks. Nole tried to hide the sly smile on his lips, but it had gone noticed by both Gabriel and I. We raised our eyebrows at the obvious attraction that the two had for each other.

"Umm…hey guys," she said looking at anywhere but Nole. "Just came by to tell you that everyone is ready and waiting downstairs."

Gabriel looked at the clock on the nightstand and muttered something underneath his breath. "How many showed up?"

Nole stepped aside to let Beth walk into the room and she shyly did so, her steps slow and uncertain. She was very beautiful in the silk light blue dress she wore that hugged her curves without showing too much. A light brown belt gingerly tied around her waist accenting her small frame. Her golden blond hair fell loosely around her in soft natural waves. The heels she wore made her significantly taller, but not too tall where it would look odd. No wonder Nole had stilled upon seeing her. She was definitely not the Beth we'd all had grown to see on a day to day basis.

"Umm...Kimberly," I hid a smile that started to form at the mention of her name. "Lucas..." Inwardly, I rolled my eyes at the sound of his name. I didn't even know why I disliked the guy so much. He'd never done anything to me.

Kimberly. That's all the reason you need.

"...and you guys."

I furrowed my eyebrows, not following her list of names after the first two. I looked at Gabriel as he nodded, taking his black jacket off of the bed, and walking towards the door. Beth followed after him with Nole and me trailing behind them.

"Pretty good turnout." I heard Gabriel say to Beth. "Plus, saves money in my pocket." He added jokingly. "I hope the cab is here because I am starving."

"Me too." We said chiming in.

Getting closer to the entrance of the castle I heard distant voices coming from the foyer. Nole and Beth were engaged in a conversation in front of me and I observed how close together the two were; their arms brushing against each other's and the extra bounce to their step, made it impossible to ignore their high spirits.

Entering the foyer I was completely mesmerized as I laid eyes on only her. I froze in my place as everything around me faded into the background, and it was just me and her in this fragment of time. She was wearing a plum – almost black – dress with ruffles that started at her waist. The dress ended an inch above her knees and drew attention to her long sexy legs. Her makeup was dark, but not to the extent that it overwhelmed her beautiful milky skin. The makeup highlighted her eyes, bringing out the clear and piercing blue in them. Kimberly's long blond hair was fashioned in soft waves just like Beth's was, and made me wonder if the two had helped each other prepare for tonight. She wore sparkly jewelry that blinded my sight as the diamonds hit the light whenever she moved...enthralling, captivating...

I felt someone grasp my shoulder, snapping me out of the trance that had held me with a hard and unyielding hand. I glanced to my left, seeing Gabriel with a light smile on his face. He nudged me and I nudged him back, urging him with my eyes to quit drawing attention to us, but that was too late.

Kimberly's eyes found me first and I saw as her face contorted into something like surprise but it quickly dissolved into nothingness, cutting me up inside. She averted her eyes from mine and turned her back at me, immersing herself in whatever conversation Lucas and Jessie were having.

"Hey, you guys get over here. I want to take a picture of everyone!" Beth said, motioning us to come hither. "Okay. Gabriel, stand near Jessie and Nole...good." She said getting them into the perfect position. "Hmm...Lucas...stand near Jessie...yes, perfect! Now, Calder and Kim stand there...will you guys smile? Sheesh!"

I cleared my throat and Kimberly shuffled her weight from one foot to the other in obvious discomfort. "Aww..." Beth muttered. "Cal and Kim are cut off...I'll take a picture of you guys after you them. 'Kay?" We nodded and she asked the others, "Ready?"

"Ready," they said in unison with genuine smiles plastered on their faces.

Kimberly and I made a move to step aside, but Beth was on us like a wild lion catching its prey. "If you guys are trying to get away...it's useless. C'mon. It'll be quick, please."

"Fine," we muttered. Beth clapped her hands and snapped a quick and awkward picture of us. I certainly wasn't smiling and judging by the frown on Beth's face, Kimberly hadn't either.

"Well, I tried." She sighed.

I turned to Gabriel and he just shrugged, crossing his hands over his chest in a 'I don't know what to tell you' gesture. I didn't know what to tell myself. Why was she acting that way? Had I done something to make her hate my guts? What had I done wrong? Why did I even care about what she thought of me?

Calder Montgomery never once cared about anyone else's opinion. Ever. So why did the only thought I cared about belong to her?

Café Moderne was certainly a luxurious but very modern restaurant – hence the name. The place was lively and very welcoming as our waiter showed us to our table sprawled with white linen table cloths and a number of wine glasses set on each table.

Good. I'll definitely need something to drink.

The tables were for two people only, but as a request from Gabriel the tables had been pushed together to look like one long table seated for a party of seven. Meaning there was only one man out or should I say woman. Jessie was the only one who didn't have someone sitting across from her at the opposite end of where I sat. Even with three people separating us I could still feel her hard cold stare on me, making me uncomfortable for most of the night.

The restaurant served a five course meal, and by dessert I was already on my ninth bottle of champagne. I was receiving questioning stares from the waiters, but since I was legal and not causing a disturbance – they turned a blind eye to the overwhelming amount of alcohol I'd consume. Gabriel leaned in and in a hard whisper said, "Your drawing attention. I think you should stop."

I waved away his concern and sipped my glass of champagne casually. Two tables over, I saw Kimberly looking at me, shaking her head in disappointment as she threw down her napkin and excused herself from the table. Lucas' eyebrows furrowed in confusion, but didn't make a move to follow her and neither did anyone else.

Pensively, I watched the clock on the faraway wall until I noticed that it had been three minutes since she left. I didn't want to draw attention to myself if I left as soon as she did. This way there was a time difference between our leaving. Standing up from the table, I made my way towards the washrooms where I thought Kimberly would be. Just as I'd expected she was leaning against a wall, her head slowly tilting back and forth as it hit the wall rhythmically.

Approaching her cautiously, I leaned against the wall next to her without saying a single word. She didn't stop hitting her head against the wall or acknowledge my presence. We stayed

like that for a very long minute, letting the comfortable silence
envelop us until she said in resignation, "What do you want
Calder?"

Ignoring her question I said, "It seems to me like your avoiding me."

"I am."

"Why?"

She turned her head to look at me, her eyes weary and glassy
in the dim lighting. "If you really have to ask that then you are
more oblivious than I thought."

She stepped forward but I quickly turned and put my arm on
one side of her – my hand resting on the wall, while my body
blocked out any means of escape. Her blue eyes widened and I
saw the conflict within; an internal battle waging behind them.
I felt her breath on my skin, hot – sending small shivers down
my spine. My eyes idly wondered to her soft pink lips – smelling
of faint watermelon just like the day in the garden. She reached
out her hand to my lips – her fingertips only a fragment of an
inch away from touching them. The closeness of our bodies was
too much to bear and I saw it in her intense blue eyes that it was
the same for her.

"Leave me alone," her breath came out shallow as if she'd
been running a marathon instead of just standing here with me.
"Please." Her hand dropped to her side, turning her face away
from me in the process.

"Not until you tell me why you're avoiding me."

"Calder, please. Just leave me alone."

"No, I need-" I heard the sound of someone clearing their
throat, loudly – distracting me from what I was about to say. I

spun around and met Lucas standing a few feet away from us, his body tense, fists clenched to his sides.

"I think she's asked you nicely to leave her alone." Cursing, I lowered my arm and turned around to face his stormy light green eyes.

"You should learn to stay out of other people's business." I snarled back.

Lucas stepped forward until there was only a visible line of space between our chests. There was tension in our position, both glaring, both feigning for a calmness that would not come. His face was too close for comfort and I waited for him to back away because I sure as hell wasn't backing down. His was voice was clipped as he said, "Stay. Away. From. Her."

"You don't own her. She's not a piece of property that you can-" He swung and I ducked out of the way before his fist connected with my face.

It was a pretty low blow, wanting to catch me off guard. That was a mistake on his part. I was never off guard. I was always waiting, calculating my opponent for their weakness. He was too slow. His rage was controlling his mind and was inaccurate as he tried to land a blow to my stomach. I ducked effortlessly, and sweep kicked him, making him fall backwards.

I grinned and pressed forward, landing a blow to his stomach, sending him backwards with its force. I threw myself forward at him, while Kimberly could only stare with panic in her eyes at the all out brawl.

He grunted with my jab and retaliated with an equal blow that sent me reeling a few steps back. I landed one last blow to his face, hearing the crunch of bones breaking as my fist connected with his nose, before Nole and Gabriel grabbed us, trying to pull us apart. Blood began to drip from the wound, seeping his white shirt with heavy red drops. Kimberly gasped and ran to his side, cradling his head in her hands. My heart slowed as I saw her choosing him over me - the world fading away, leaving me to endure this moment over and over again like a million shards piercing my chest.

Gabriel let me go as soon as he realized that I wouldn't beat the crap out of the guy, but Kimberly wasn't finished with me as she yelled, "Why don't you pick on someone your own size, you big jerk!"

I snapped out of my thoughts and blankly looked up at her, but quickly pulled a mask of indifference over my face. I rolled my eyes at her accusation. Lucas had seen worst and the bastard deserved it. I was only defending myself, and least of all people she should know that. He would heal in a matter of minutes without a scratch to indicate a fight. She still wasn't familiar with how our world worked and was...wait. Did she just call me big?

"Are you calling me fat?"

She shook her head. "No..."

"Yes, you are. You just called me fat!"

"I didn't call you fat!" She yelled in exasperation.

"It was implied." I said curtly. She took out a handkerchief from her purse and used it to soak up the blood from his nose. The wound was already healing in front of our eyes, but she continued to fuss over his well being.

Spectators had gathered around to see what the commotion was about. They whispered in hush tones at the mess we'd created. Beth's eyes were wide with horror as she saw the blood on Lucas' shirt, while Gabriel and Nole were both giving us worried side glances as they stood near us in case another altercation broke out. Jessie was the least shocked, and a brief read of her mind showed that she was expecting this from me.

"Well, you're not fat." Kimberly answered, leaving Lucas on the ground to Beth and Nole as she walked towards me, her eyes seething with anger.

Out of the corner of my eye I saw a waiter heading our way, and decided that I would leave without having to be told to do so. Giving her a sardonic smile I said, "It's about time you realized that Kimberly."

A flash of light caught my attention and I saw a reporter - standing in the middle of the restuarant, taking pictures of me and the scene I was leaving behind as I walked out of the doors.

CHAPTER 9

"What were you thinking? What was going on inside your mind to have caused you to act in that way, Cal? Are you mentally incapable of refraining from attacking someone?"

Gabriel roared. He was pissed and when he was angry he ranted, while pacing back and forth the vicinity of the room.

Nole was sitting on his bed, casually lying down as he stared up at the ceiling. A quick read of his mind voiced the same questions and allegations that Gabriel was saying. He wondered what could have set me off to have fought with Lucas almost beating the living crap out of him. If it wasn't for Gabe and me...I don't think he would have stopped.

Nole was right. I don't believe I would have stopped if they hadn't showed up.

"Oh! And not just anyone," Gabriel continued, flinging his hands up in exasperation. "No...Calder Montgomery had to fight with a fellow Keeper, a fellow brother! For what? Why did that fight occur 'cause I sure as hell don't have the slightest idea other than the obvious. But the Calder I know would never in his right mind fight for something that trivial."

"I know!" I snapped. "I lost control. Sorry."

"That's it?!" He whirled around facing me, his eyes a torturous stormy gray. Damn. He was really pissed. "That's all you have to say for yourself. It's not me you should be apologizing too, it's Lucas."

"What?" I stood up clenching my jaw. "He's the one who started the fight anyway. I was only acting in self-defense and if you were there you would know that instead of jumping to conclusions!"

He sighed in frustration, grabbing his hair and pulling at it. "You shouldn't have been involved in an altercation with him. You could have held him off just as easily without beating the crap out of him. That's my point."

He was right. I could have restrained him, but that was the easy way. Gabe should know that I didn't take the easy route when it came to solving a problem. The solution to solving Lucas' interference was to teach him a lesson my way.

"What am I going to do about this now?" Gabriel muttered, slumping down onto his bed. He sighed, flopping on his back crossly.

"Nothing." I said.

He scoffed. "Easy for you to say. You'll have to get a mark on your record for this. You know fighting with another is against our code. We aren't supposed to waste our time fighting with one another over mundane things, but-"

"But fighting against the evils of the world." I finished. It was one of our mantras that were engraved in my head. I sighed knowing that Gabriel was right. "Fine. Report it to our fathers. It's my first time and I'll probably just get off with a warning."

There was no response from him and I let the quietness come as a comfort that this discussion was over. I hadn't even been inside our room for five minutes before he came storming in and accusing me for what happened at the restaurant to be my fault. Sure, it had been my fault but not entirely. If Lucas hadn't shown up to stick his nose into places where it did not belong then we never would have had a problem. But things were never easy. Life was never easy. Someone always ruined a perfectly good moment.

I took of my shoes and began to undress when suddenly an alarm started to sound, ringing in my ears. Immediately, I was alert and so were Gabriel and Nole as they leaped out of their beds and headed towards the door. I quickly put my shows back on followed suit, buttoning my shirt in the process. I found the hallway filled with our novices, confusion and alarm written all over their faces. They were preparing for bed as some were dressed in their pj's while others were still wearing their casual wear. Looking around, I saw that the other Keepers in our council were running towards the foyer and I was the last of us left.

I ran into Beth on my way out and then saw Kimberly emerge behind her; panic visible in their eyes. I stopped and lowered myself so that I was at eye level with Beth. "I want you to go back into your room and tell the others to stay there. Got it?"

She nodded her head. "What's happening?"

"Don't worry about it, kid. Just some Keeper business to take care of – don't worry. Just get back inside."

She reluctantly nodded, walking back into her room. Kimberly was a different matter all together. She must have seen something in my face that caused her alarm. "You're lying. It's more than that. I can help." She reached out to put her hand on my shoulder but stopped midair thinking better of the gesture.

"I'm sorry. You're still a novice, Kim. Stay with Beth and if you see the others tell them to stay in their rooms. That's an order." She nodded her head slowly, but I saw the determination in her eyes to have been given something to do.

Without another word I sprinted down the hallway and met up with the rest of the Keepers, full pledged and all. I cluttered among my fellow brothers and sisters, listening to an older Keeper whose voice rose above the alarm that was ringing. His voice must have been a spell cast to amplify his voice because it couldn't have been humanly possible for it to be that loud.

"There are a group of demons outside, attacking the barrier outside the castle. That is the cause of the alarm. We have detected them to be Lazrith demons." He said, his voice composed and commanding. "I know you may all be wondering about the activity and classify it as unnatural. It is. But it has happened before as many of you would recall."

I saw the shaking of heads as they agreed, but others were confused about the new information as I was. I had previously read about demons banding together centuries ago, but the cause for it was never written down. There was something more to it than they were letting on... "I need all of the Keepers who are magic yielders to come to me now as the rest of you will return to your rooms."

It was an order. As much as I wanted to go up to this Keeper and tell him that I could help I knew that it wouldn't have done any good. I saw Gabriel step forward, meeting with Lily and the others who shared their gift. They would probably be used to sustain the barrier surrounding the castle since the damage that the demons were creating would fracture the spell originally placed. I thought it strange that they wouldn't have sent us to fight and kill the bloody beasts for once and for all. Maybe that was a job for their Keepers.

This is a matter of our own to handle...

Elder Dupont's words echoed over and over again in my mind like a broken record. I wondered if this wasn't the first that something like this has occurred here. It was uncommon and outright foolish for demons to attack at a central council command center. Surely they must know that they are up against odds here where hundreds of Keepers are here. It just didn't make any kind of sense.

Everything that I had learned about demon kinds, behavior, patterns, and habitat was being torn apart. This didn't happen and I needed to know why the sudden change. Gabriel had been right to suspect this kind of thing as being wrong. I felt it. I felt it at the pit of my stomach, telling me that there was a bigger picture. There was never a reason why demons had began to band together and attack, bringing dozens of Keepers lives to an end. It was a secret long ago buried and only the ones who were alive knew the answer.

Reluctantly, I turned around and joined the Keepers who had been ordered to return to their chambers. Looking back, I saw Keepers rushing back and forth in the foyer, preparing for battle.

They were gathering weapons, setting them down in the middle of the room. I kept walking but the sound of metal against metal traveled throughout the corridor, taunting me to turn back and argue my way into fighting alongside the French Keepers.

Before I could go back I found myself standing in front of the door I saw Beth and Kimberly come out of and decided in that moment to look after them. If Gabriel was the one in my place he would check on them and explain the situation as best he could. That's the least I could do. The French Council wouldn't provide answers even if I asked because I wasn't one of them.

As Dupont had said it was 'a matter of our own to handle.'

Pushing the thoughts aside I knocked softly on their door. In seconds it opened and my gray-blue eyes met Kimberly's soft blue ones. She bites her lip anxiously and I notice the worry etched in her brow as she looks around for any signs of anyone else. "Is everything okay?"

Instead of answering her question I asked, "Can I come in?"

Kimberly opened the door wider and stepped to the side to let me pass. Beth saw me, jumping out of bed, and leaping into my arms. I caught her taken aback by her enthusiasm or maybe it was worry laced with enthusiasm? I wasn't sure but I welcomed the familiarity of it.

"I'm glad you're okay! There are demons outside! I saw them from the window." I pulled her back and saw the fear in her eyes and noticed the tremble to her voice even when she tried to hide it. She was strong but it was nerve wrecking the first time we lay eyes on a demon. "Wh-what are they doing here?"

"I don't know. But I believe that they are working on the barrier to protect everyone here."

"They aren't sending Keepers out to fight?" Kimberly asked astounded. I shook my head. "But that's...ridiculous!" Her hands went up in the air in frustration and at the same time she kicked the front of her bed post. "We should be out their fighting! There aren't many of them so why don't they send some of their Keepers out? It doesn't make any kind of sense."

"Tell me about it." I muttered. "It's the same thing I thought."

"Why did you come back?" Beth asked looking at me curiously.

"I wasn't needed. Gabriel and Lily are the only one of us who went with them to help. They are the only one of us have magic yielding abilities. We would be of no use to them."

She nodded understandingly and I heard Kimberly mutter, "So Lucas didn't go. I should go see if he's alright."

I rolled my eyes and couldn't help but blurt out, "Why do you care so much about him? You act like he's some defenseless animal who can't take care of himself." My voice was cold and I hated how I acted when his name was brought up. This wasn't me. This wasn't who I am.

It is you. She has done this to you, but you're just too stubborn to admit it. You're afraid...

I closed my eyes, taking a deep breath and pushing those thoughts into the deepest corner of my mind. There was a time and place for them and this was definitely not the time to indulge in them.

I heard a sharp intake of breath and I snapped my eyes open. Beth was sucking in her cheeks and looking at me with wide eyes. Kimberly was frozen in her spot, her back rigid as she turned to look at me. She bit her lip and looked down at her shoes trying to hide the blush that crept to her cheeks. It was not the expression that I would have thought to arise from her. I imagined her eyes flashing with anger, but instead she was embarrassed.

"I-I," She stuttered and I thought that it was kind of cute. From all the time that I'd known her she was never the one at a loss for words. That had been me. "It's not that. He's my-"

"Boyfriend," I cut in. "I know. Still don't get why you treat him like a little puppy that can't take care of himself. He's a Keeper." I said harshly. "He doesn't need to be babied by some girl."

"You think Lucas is my...wait. What?" She said, laughing. "He's more of a man than you'll ever be."

"What's that supposed to mean?"

"Are you ever going to apologize for hitting him?" She asked, putting her hands on her hips.

"Oh, I don't know. Are you going to apologize for calling me fat?" I countered.

She flung her hands up in the air and said to Beth, "Can you believe him?" Beth was trying not to laugh but I didn't know what was so amusing. To me Kimberly said, "I believe I said a big jerk, not a fat jerk."

"So you admit!"

She rolled her eyes and slumped down on the same bed that Beth occupied. "Unbelievable." She lifted her arm up to her face to cover her eyes in a distress manner. Like the kind of gesture you see a damsel in distress make when she's asking for help. "You punch a guy and you're worried about your gut."

"Well, not-"

There was a knock at the door and I prayed to not let it be Lucas. Someone must have been listening because I opened it to find Nole standing lazily in the empty corridor. His hands were in his pockets and there was a hesitant smile on his face that quickly turned to confusion.

I stepped aside and let him in, answering the question that's on his mind. "Just came to check on them and see if they were alright. Why are you here?"

Nole glanced at Beth and then answered, "The same."

Ha. That was a lie. He came for Beth, apparently they were going to meet up later tonight and take a walk down the maze like path in the gardens. That much I had gathered from reading his mind in all about five seconds. Nole walked to one of the bigger windows in the room and looked outside as I followed suit. Beth and Kimberly quickly came to stand beside us as we watched the activity outside grow at an alarming rate as the minutes turned to hours.

The demons were relentless as they clawed at the barrier trying to break down its magic. It wasn't strong enough even with many of the magic yielders power sustaining the barrier. It wasn't enough. Constantly having to uphold the barrier took a large amount of strength and it must have been tiring them. The only possible option to solve the problem was to go out and fight the Lazrith demons. That's what should have been done in the first place. Why they didn't was beyond me.

It was almost three hours since the breech occurred and I was becoming restless. It wasn't in my character to stand along the sidelines and not do anything while we were being attacked. Every bone in my body screamed to run out there and kill the blood bastards. I wasn't the only one who felt that way. I saw the tension in Nole's back as he too was fighting the instinct inside. Kimberly also looked like she wanted to do something as she paced back and forth in the small room, but quit as it caused her to become dizzy.

"Come look!" Beth exclaimed suddenly. We had all tired and were sprawled across the room, lost in our own thoughts. I had chosen a corner and sat down on the floor concentrating on Gabriel's mind. He was using his magic as I had thought, drawing his inner strength from within to hold the barrier together. He was becoming weak and I felt how his life force was draining. He needed to rest soon or he would lose consciousness in a matter of minutes.

Hearing Beth's voice snapped me out of his mind and I returned to my own. I blinked away my slightly blurred vision and took a moment to collect myself. Standing up, I saw the others had already joined Beth by the window and there were small gasps from the girls as I approached.

The sight I saw outside was breath taking for someone who had never seen a battle to this extent. There were demons catching fire and the clattering of metal meeting the hard, razor sharp spikes on the Lazrith demons. There must have been at least fifty Keepers out on the lawn fighting the lizard-like demons. I knew that all of them belonged to the French Council and were fully pledged Keepers by their form of fighting. They fought using their heart rather than their mind as the French were so commonly known for. When fighting it was best to use logic and strategy not emotion as it would get you killed.

I observed the rustling of trees to the right side of the woods and that's when I saw more of them appear. It was an ambush. It had all been a trap.

In that moment I understood why the council had ordered magic yielders to work on the barriers. They knew. They somehow knew that this would happen.

We all watched as the number of Lazrith demons grew and more Keepers were dispatched to fight. Demons fell as they were decapitated and burned to nothing but ashes to show their existence. Pyrokinesis using Keepers were the majority out on the ground fighting. Their ability to manipulate the fire to their will was extraordinary as demons fell to the ground and burned to nothing but ashes; the fire dancing as it caught the evil in its fiery hand.

But even though we had the upper hand, and knew deep down that we would defeat the evil creatures -it didn't mean that there were no casualties. I saw as some Keepers went down, wounded by the Lazrith demon's venom they carried in their claws. The venom worked its way into our body, slowly shutting down our nervous system until we collapsed. Healing worked but it took hours for our body to self-generate and recover – that is if the demon didn't kill us first. I closed my eyes as I couldn't bear to watch the demons sink their teeth into the fallen Keepers, clawing their flesh and ripping their heads clean off from their shoulders.

I moved away from the window, sitting down on one of the beds. I put my head in my hands as the feeling of weakness washed over me. I hated sitting here and watching my fellow brothers and sisters out there fighting, while I was here doing nothing. Nothing. I needed to be out there just like I needed the air to breath.

There was movement next to me and I felt the pressure of the bed lower as someone sat next to me. I didn't have to look to see who it was. The air around me began to smell faintly of watermelon.   I knew exactly who it was by the soft touch of her hand on my knee, sending small spasms of heat through my body.

"Don't blame yourself. This isn't your fault." She said softly, her words meaning more to me than she would ever know.

I looked up to face her soft and kind face. "I still wish I could do something. Anything."

"You're here with us. That's something, Calder." She smiled reassuringly. I nodded and saw her expression change into a sly grin as she added, "That's enough, even if you are a big jerk."

I chucked and she joined in as our laughter filled the room. Beth and Nole turned to us, appalled expressions on their faces. "What on earth is so funny?" Beth asked grieved.

Kimberly and I exchanged glances and muffled our laughter but failed. Nole and Beth exchanged a glance of their own that soon turned into ear to ear smiles, sharing a conspiratorial gleam all the while. Kim and I looked at each other and shrugged not knowing what they were so happy about it.

That's what we tried to do for the remainder of the night. We tried to take each other's minds off the battle going on outside of our window. As the night turned to dawn, the fight outside subsided at the first rays of sunlight crept over the horizon.

I looked down at the lawn and saw about a dozen or so fallen bodies. There were more scorch marks than dead Keepers and so that meant we won. We won. Whatever they were after they weren't successful in accomplishing it. There was something of importance here, something of value to them and they would stop at nothing to get their hands on it. The question was: What did they want?

Kimberly stirred on the bed beside me. She and Beth had fallen asleep in the early hours of the morning. They didn't want to go to bed while Nole and I were still awake, and were stubborn until Kimberly passed out on the floor and I carried her to her bed. Beth was a determined little thing and only began to sink into sleep when Nole sat next to her on the bed holding her hand. It was a sight to see how relaxed and tender he became when he was with her. He cared for her that much I knew by appearance alone. I didn't have the nerve to pry into his mind and read his feelings for Beth.

Love wasn't my forte and I wasn't going to become a victim by it. Not after seeing the haunted look in my father's eyes every day; something that my mother's death had caused. Then there was Gabriel and how broken he was inside by losing Gwen. His case was different but in the end it was the same result. He still lost the only person he loved and probably would ever love. He could never be with her. I didn't want that. I couldn't let that happen to me.

Nothing was worth being in love if that was the price in the end. That's what love causes. Love destroys. You give your heart – you're entire being to another person and once they leave it feels like you've died along with them. You can love for a second and feel the pain of loss for a lifetime. I didn't need love and I certainly didn't want it. I had everything I needed.

"Calder?"

I turned, shaking away my thoughts and looked down at Kim's sleepy gaze. I kneeled beside Kimberly's bed as she wiped the sleep from her eyes, the sun casting a glow around her, making her look unearthly like angel as her hair was a golden halo around her. "Is it over?" She asked groggily.

I nodded as I placed my hand on her cheek, tenderly. "Sleep. We're safe now." She slightly nodded and closed her eyes to welcome dreams once more. I began to stand up but she reached out her hand and caught the sleeve off my jacket.

"Stay." It wasn't a question or a plea, but a simple word that beckoned me to do as she said. I found myself sinking down to the floor, my chin resting on the edge of the bed as I watched her sleep. Her chest rising as she took deep, slow even breaths. It took every ounce of self control to not reach out and stroke her hair as she lay there dreaming of fairytales that I could never be.

She deserved better. She deserved someone who could return her love. Not someone who was afraid of it.

Chapter 10

I had fallen asleep beside Kimberly's bed and was woken up when the girls began to get ready for the brand new day ahead. As I watched Kim gather her things to get dressed, there was a pang inside my chest at the conflicting thoughts my mind had against my heart. My decision was final and no matter what my feelings were they couldn't continue. They were merely going to remain as that: feelings.

She needed someone that was capable of love and a boy who lived up to her expectations. I was neither of those things. Lucas was it, and I couldn't stand in their way of happiness.

Nole and I headed to our room, the afternoon sun beaming through the corridor windows, casting light through the eerie dark hall. Entering our chamber, we found Gabriel packing. He was idly tossing all his belongings in his suitcase in a fit of anger. He was absentmindedly muttering to himself, but was too low for me to hear and guess as to what he was upset about.

I was concerned about his well-being – my earlier feelings evaporating and were replaced with worry for Gabriel's sake. I saw that he hadn't fully recovered from his extensive use of magic last night by the weariness in his eyes. His skin was pale and his eyes rimmed with dark shadows underneath them. He must have rested to recover his strength back but he hadn't sleep in over twenty-four hours. He was drained, but also frustrated about something.

"What's going on?" Nole asked. "Are we leaving?"

"Yes. Pack your things. We're to leave immediately."

His voice was hard, as he ransacked the remainder of the closet, tossing our clothes on the bed. He moved to the bathroom next and began to clear all our belongings. He dumped the contents onto the bed and took a step to collect more of our effects, but I stopped him.

"What is going on?" I said, repeating Nole's question. "Why are we leaving? We've only been here for a day. Is it because of the attack from last night?"

"Yes." He said. "We aren't welcomed here anymore. Dupont wants us to return home to our council."

"What's his reasoning?"

"Didn't give me one."

I stared at him blankly. That didn't make sense. Why wasn't anything making sense? "He just told you that we needed to leave?"

"Pretty much." He zipped up his suit case, heading towards the door. He turned around, dejected as he said, "I'm going to go tell the others. We've got one hour to return home. I've already reached our fathers to tell them the news. They'll talk to us when we get home."

I was going to offer to tell everyone the news, but he was gone before I could utter a word. Nole and I exchanged a concerned look for Gabriel, but left it at that. There was no need to voice the questions we both had. They were the same questions that plagued our thoughts from the night before. Something was wrong here. Things were changing.

The council chamber was empty except for Calder, Elder Montgomery, my father, and me. As soon as we'd arrived back home, Cal and I headed straight to the chamber to meet them and I again informed them of the events that transpired the night before. There was a brief moment of silence before my father spoke in the quiet room.

"It is not of our concern what the French Council is hiding as you so blatantly put it. We only get involved when they ask for our help, son."

"But you can't deny that something is wrong here. Demons are attacking in packs." Calder said looking at his father and then at mine. "There is something going on here. We heard that this has happened centuries ago but there is no record of why and you told us to come to you if we heard of anymore demonic activity. That is what we are doing and I don't know why we aren't taking action to stop it from continuing."

I hid the grin forming on my face as best I could. Calder wasn't one for subtlety and this was the perfect example. Our fathers exchanged a grieved look with one another, but it was gone in seconds as fast as it had come, replaced with calmness and composure.

"There are secrets as ancient as the foundation of our world," Elder Montgomery said standing up from his seat and heading over to the many bookshelves that surrounded the council chamber. "Secrets that are reserved for when you come of age and you take your pledge."

"What is happening with the demons has happened before many centuries ago." My father said, sighing. "I'm sorry to say this but it is neither of your concern. You must let it be for now. We will take care of it."

"You just want us to stand by and watch this continue rather than getting to the bottom of it?" Calder exclaimed.

My father nodded his head solemnly. "For now you will continue your duties as before, but the number of Keepers dispatched on missions will increase. With these new revelations we cannot take chances in casualties."

"If you know what's causing this then why don't we go to the source and stop it?" I asked disregarding what he just said. I wanted answers. Need them. None of this made sense. It wasn't what I had learned throughout these past few years. Apparently, there were exceptions.

"We need time," was all that my father said.

Calder rolled his eyes, sighing in frustration. "This is ridiculous!"

"Calder!"

He spun around facing his father with a maddening gaze that could cause discomfort in anyone else, but not in his own father. Elder Montgomery was not afraid of his own son's rage. "Mind your tongue. We are having a discussion and there is no need for your childish defiance."

Calder clenched his jaw, biting at the retort he must have had. I was just as angry about this situation, but I knew when to speak and when it wasn't appropriate. "So there's no use in trying to get answers from either of you." I said factually rather than asking.

"No. There are still rules to uphold. Both of you will know when you pass through the rite. All will be revealed then. For now, continue to train the novices with your fellow Keepers." My father said in the powerful voice that indicated he was in Elder mode. His voice was commanding, grabbing the attention of everyone in the room. He cleared his throat, seemingly embarrassed at the switch of manners, and casted a glance at Elder Montgomery. He nodded, a silent understanding passing with one another.

My dad and Cal's dad were a lot like us. They had been best friends since they were fourteen. The same age that Cal and I met. It certainly was a sight to see how they regarded each other as equals. Even though my father was the head of the council he still confided and regarded Mr. Montgomery on matters of importance, or matters concerning their sons. It was a bit disconcerting, imagining myself and Cal in their position one day.

"We apologize that your week off has been ruined." My father said solemnly. I crossed my arms over my chest, guessing where the turn of conversation was heading. We were done discussing the secret that we weren't privy to and on to matters that involved our responsibility.

"We did believe that you all deserved it seeing the amount of improvement all the novices have made, but in light of things, you will continue training as of tomorrow."

"Clearly." Calder muttered, looking at his feet.

"What was that, Calder?"

He snapped his head up and met his father's sharp gaze. "Nothing."

"Good," was all Mr. Montgomery said. He started making his way back to his seat but stopped short, saying, "The ball."

"Oh, yes. Matters of the ball." Calder and I looked at each other, confusion flickering on our faces. You think they'd cancel it? Calder asked telepathically.

Don't know. They might.

But it's tradition. You don't think they'd actually cancel it, do you?

I don't know, I paused, thinking. I don't know what to think anymore. Everything has changed.

"We haven't discussed the matter with the other council members but it looks like we will be having the annual Midnight Masked Ball. We can't stop tradition and as you know it is one of our most sacred customs."

We nodded, knowing fairly well what he meant. The Midnight Masked Ball was held three days prior to Christmas and was a celebration of when we received our magical gifts from a higher being. As centuries passed instead of it being a ritual of sorts it changed to a grand ball full of costumes, dancing, food, and mysteries. Strange happenings occurred on that night. There were some Keepers who would wake up the next day without any recollection of the night's events or sightings of ghosts in corridors.

I smiled, remembering the light that had appeared to me twice before and felt delight in its presence whenever it materialized. I was certain that it was a ghost that needed my help even if Calder didn't share the same sentiment.

Thinking of who you'll be taking there, Gabe?

I chuckled, my shoulders shaking with effort to hold my laughter within. No, but I bet your thinking of asking Kimberly.

I looked up and saw Calder stiffen, his eyes holding the slightest hint of pain...? He turned away from me, clearing his throat to hide the feelings going through his mind. "Are we done here?" He asked abruptly.

My father looked up, eyebrows furrowed in confusion and slowly said, "Yes. Both of you may be excused."

Calder turned on his heels and was almost out the door before his father caught his elbow. "There's no need to think that way Calder. Don't justify your feelings solely on what you see, but about how you feel, son."

"I don't know what you're talking about." He said coldly, yanking his arm away from his father's grasp. "Whatever it is there is no need to speak about it."

"There is, Calder." Mr. Montgomery said gravely. His eyes took on a distant look, caught up in a memory. "We need to talk about it sometime. Now, seems the appropriate time."

I looked at my father, searching his eyes for answers but found none. Sometimes I really wished that I had received mind reading as one of my gifts. It would make knowing everyone's thoughts so much easier and I'd gain knowledge of thoughts I wasn't privy too as Calder did. I wondered what the conflict between Calder and Mr. Montgomery was. There was something deeper than Calder's feelings, which I guessed that Mr. Montgomery felt if they were strong enough. By the dead lock gaze that father and son held it was clear that Mr. Montgomery had felt exactly what his son was feeling.

Calder stepped away from his father, shaking his head in disbelief. "No. I don't want to see the anguish on your face when you speak of her. I don't want to be like you."

I gaped; shocked that Calder would say something as cold as that to his father. Hurt flashed in Mr. Montgomery eyes, and he stepped forward meeting his son's hard gaze. The atmosphere in the room changed into a thick layer of uneasiness and tension. It was like watching a horror film, waiting for the moment where the killer was going to appear behind the main character, ready to kill them. That's how it felt seeing Calder and Mr. Montgomery's intense locked gaze; waiting for what was to come next.

Slowly, Mr. Montgomery shook his head. There was sadness in his gray-blue eyes; the same eyes that mirrored his son's. "The past is the past," Mr. Montgomery said. "But what you make of the future is in your hands. You can't let the past frighten you. That's not reason enough to feel a vital part of life."

Calder scoffed. "And what might that be?"

I sucked in a deep breath, an idea forming in my head of what may have caused Calder's sudden cold demeanor and Mr. Montgomery's sullen one. A sharp pain began to form in my chest and I grasped the chain around my neck, somewhat calming the ache within.

I looked at my father, a small smile forming on his lips and I looked back to see a similar smile on Mr. Montgomery's mouth. "Love, Calder. You can't shut love out. It's as much of us as the air we breathe and the magic within us."

"You're wrong." Calder said through clenched teeth. There was a twitch at the side of his jaw, hinting at the emotions he was trying to hide. "Love destroys. I've seen it happened more than once." He stepped back, heading towards the door, but before he exited he casted a glance at me. I saw the slightest trace of guilt and dejection in his eyes before he was gone and through the door - a loud echo resonated within the chamber, marking his exit.

Seeing the brief pain in his eyes made me realize who he meant when he said that love destroys. He was talking about his father and the other person was me.

I began to take my leave, touching the chain around my neck, thinking about the girl I left behind those many years ago – the girl who holds my heart yet has no knowledge that she does. Calder was wrong. Love doesn't destroy. It may cause pain because you miss the other person, but it doesn't destroy you. There is just the longing left inside, yearning for the opportunity to see each other again and spend time with them no matter how brief or extensive it may be.

We might live for centuries, but that didn't mean that we should waste the time we had. Calder was foolish to think that he could survive without love. He was foolish to think that he could control his feelings for Kimberly. He was an idiot for thinking that such a thing like love was a curse, a disease.

He had his own reasons for his thoughts and I had mine. But having firsthand experience of what love feels like, I can certainly vouch that it does not destroy. Sometimes, it's the only thing that keeps you intact, keeps you alive for the years ahead.

Love saves us and gives us the strength to carry on when we least expect it.

CHAPTER 11

Exhaustion washed over me as I watched the last rays of light vanish over the horizon and dusk settled, casting the garden in an amber glow. The garden was where I went to when I needed to take my mind of off things. I ignored Gabriel's telepathic calls (as I liked to call them) for hours until he gave up entirely, and I didn't hear him in my head any longer. When a person focused all their thoughts into getting a hold of me and if the connection was strong enough then they could easily send a message, which I could interfere. It was like having my own frequency and only a strong connection could get through to me.

Gabriel was the only one who had ever tried to communicate with me and succeeded. It was no easy feat and I commended him for it, but at the moment I was not to keen on him trying to get a hold of me. I wanted to be left alone, and didn't need him to talk to me. I already knew what he would say by the thoughts circulating in his mind. I didn't need to hear it from him as well.

The moon was beginning to rise; a giant orange oval on the horizon that vaguely reminded me of the sun as it cast its rays as dawn approached. It always amazed me how the moon was orange when it first rose, and as it slowly crept up to the sky it turned silver-white, illuminating the world below. I watched the moon steadily rise until it was high in the vast sky, surrounded by the infinite number of gleaming stars.

The universe was immeasurable. There was no correct calculation of how much was out there in the world. I believed that there were many unknown treasures that still needed to be discovered, waiting for the right person to come around and see it for what it is. I wanted her to see me for who I was...

I shook my head as an effort to get rid of the thought. But as much as I tried I couldn't get away from the thought.

She saw something in me, something that no other girl had. I don't know if it was the perception in her brilliant blue (sometimes green) eyes or the quirk of her mouth that had me spellbound like no other girl had ever done before. Kimberly was different and it was why I needed to stay away from her. I couldn't screw it up and hurt her in the end. She deserved better. She deserved someone who could be there for her in ways that I know I could not provide.

It was a promise I'd made to myself a long time ago. I would not – under any circumstance – let myself fall in love with anyone. Losing Mom still haunted Dad even though it had been nearly two decades since her death. It was strange to see the grief in his eyes as it had swallowed him up, never letting him go from its tight hold enabling his life. I always questioned the idea of Dad possibly finding someone else. He was still young and could marry again if he wanted to, but he never made the effort to be with someone else like Gabriel. Why didn't they find someone else to love instead of being consumed by loss, deprived of the one thing they both needed – no, wanted?

That's what I didn't fully understand. Was it hard to fall in love again after you've had the best? What was so difficult about the bloody concept? I thought love was easy but instead it was difficult and caused your brain to melt into mush.

"Ugh!" I let out in a sigh of aggravation. Standing up, I made my way back to the castle, hiding under the protection of the shadows.

It was time to stop wallowing in my own self pity and start putting it to good use. I would take out my frustrations in the training room, rather than sit here and debate the trivial matters of women.

My knuckles were bleeding, but I didn't stop to let my body heal it. I kept on going, punching the bag in front of me imagining it was a demon that I was finishing off. I showed no mercy, throwing punch after punch as blood smeared on the bags plastic surface. Every blow was a thought I wanted erase – gone from my mind.

Judging from how long I'd been here there were a lot of things I wanted out of my head. I wanted my father and Gabriel to stop wallowing in their grief. I wanted them to find someone else to love so that the grief would forever ever leave them. I wanted Kimberly to leave and go somewhere else. She was the cause of all these feelings inside of me. The only way to solve that was for her to leave or for I to make her leave. Above all that, I wanted to stop thinking about love and what it could possibly be or mean.

Sweat beaded off of my body in waves, stinging my knuckles with the saltiness of it. No matter how much in pain my body felt, I didn't stop. I didn't want to stop. This was the only way I could stop thinking of insignificant, misconstrued thoughts. Feeling the pain physically was better than feeling any at all. If I couldn't withstand pain then I wasn't good enough. Being a Keeper meant being strong. I had to think like a warrior – logically, with my head rather than my heart. Being a Keeper meant...

"You're bleeding."

My body stilled; the punch I was going to throw forgotten as my hand dropped limply to my side. I closed my eyes, hearing the loud drumming of my heart in my ears. My breath came out in shallow labored breaths as my body uncoiled. I turned around and faced her troubled blue eyes that only grew wider as she took in my appearance.

"Here let me help you." She said, directing me to sit down next to her on the mat. A first aid kit was ready in her hands and she begun to take bandages and anti-septic cloths out of the box.

Hesitantly, I sat down across from her; all my preconceived thoughts dissipating as I watched her attentively dress my wounds. I'd done more harm than I'd realized. I could actually see the bones of my knuckles sticking out in an unnatural manner and I flinched.

"You really did it this time, Cal."

"What?"

She shook her head. "What did the punching bag ever do to you?"

"Nothing of your concern." I answered.

The corner of her mouth quirked upwards, trying for a smile but failing. She continued to tend to my hands and I watched the care in her eyes as she worked. I barely noticed the sting of the anti-septic as it touched the open skin. Since I've been a Keeper, I'd never once gotten hurt to this extent that my body wasn't properly healing on its own.

It reminded me of a story I once heard. It was our version of a horror story and it was only told when we were novices. The older Keepers would take us on a camping trip in the woods as part of our training to learn of other means of survival. We also learned basic nature survival skills like starting a fire, gathering edible food from plants, and making weapons with the available resources provided for us by Mother Nature.

On the last night of the camping trip all of us would gather around the camp fire as we heard a long ago tale of a Keeper that was kidnapped centuries ago.

His name has been lost to history and no one knew what his real name was except for those who had been alive at that time. He was kidnapped by a demon and tortured until he gave it what it wanted. The wounds that the demon inflicted caused enough damage that the Keeper couldn't regenerate, making his wounds intolerable. The pain was too much to bear and the Keeper gave the demon what it wanted. But the demon wasn't satisfied and he wanted more. The Keeper wouldn't give him anything more. He told it that he would rather die at the hands of his brothers than betray them again. So the demon did the only other thing it could.

It killed him.

They say that you could still hear his anguished screams before he died.

It's an awful way to die. Being tortured to the point where self-generation wasn't feasibly possible. I would never want to die in that way. I want my death to be quick and during battle - the less amount of pain the better.

"Okay, you're all done."

I looked down and saw one of my hands idly lying on her lap. She followed my gaze and blushed at the position of my hand, but didn't make an attempt to move it. Instead she leaned forward where there was only a visible amount of space between us. Her soft eyes traveled to my lips and I felt my heart quicken inside of my chest. The watermelon scent that I'd come to associate to her sent my nerves on end. I leaned forward, our lips brushing against each other's like a feather lightly brushing on your skin, soft and delicate. But then I said the stupidest thing I could have ever said at that moment.

"At the rate you're going between Lucas to me, people are going to question your virtue."

I mentally slapped myself. I don't know what made me say it, but the words were out of my mouth before I could stop them. Kimberly backed away from me, but not before she slapped me.

"You're an ass, have I told you that?" Her eyes shot daggers at me.

"Yes, actually you have. Not the first time you've mentioned it." She scoffed and lifted her hand up again, but I seized it before she could strike me again. "Hey," I said pulling her towards me so that I whispered in her ear. "Play nice. Now, it's very much at stake with these kinky foreplay games you've got going on here."

She clenched her teeth. "Let me go, you weak insufferable bastard. You can't even let me beat the crap out of you like you deserve."

I let her go and she backed away from me, her eyes seething with anger. There was no trace of the kindness I'd seen on her face only a few moments ago. That had passed with only rage remaining in its presence.

"You want to play games? Alright, show me what you got." I said.

I took a few steps back, allowing her to decide whether to attack me or to walk away. I watched her inquisitive eyes scan me, calculating my movements. It was then that I realized she'd chosen the former as she took a challenging step forward. Raising my eyebrow, I let her continue to advance on me until she stood a few feet from me. I didn't think she'd take the challenge and instead walk away. She had more of a backbone than I thought.

Her feet were shoulder width apart, her back erect, and her fists clenched at her sides. Pure anger and defensiveness radiated from her as she charged slowly towards me, like an animal stalking her prey. Her eyes became brazen and alive, burning with a fiery intensity that brought up the word Sexy in my mind.

I would never hit her no matter how many times she got a lucky shot in, but I wouldn't be defenseless either.

Raising her arm she threw a punch that would have connected with my jaw if I had not blocked it. It didn't faze her and she went for another punch to my stomach, but I blocked that attack too. She was no match for me. I was merely amusing her idea of beating the crap out of me as she so lightly put it. Kimberly was letting her anger get the best of her, which made her movements awkward and impulsive. It was easy enough to calculate her next move and deflect it. Her eyes gave it away the brief second it flickered to the location of her next attack. It became an elegant dance as I lead and she followed, falling into my trap every time with no clue of how to get out.

"Fine, you want to play rough–"

Tiring from the ridiculous game, I stalked forward, backing her up against the wall, pinning her with my body as she struggled to break free. She thrashed around trying to find the means to escape, but I knew better than to give her an out.

Her shoulders slacked in defeat as she realized that I had the upper hand - the game was in my territory. Kimberly's eyes took on a wounded look, going completely still in my grasp with only the sound of her shallow breathing. I smirked, leaning into her ear to whisper, "Never play grown up games when you're not up to par. I always win."

Her body shuttered beneath me, coercing a foreign sensation up my spine. I circled my fingers around her wrists and brought them above her head with one hand, a smirk twisting its way on my mouth.

She rolled her eyes and then bit her lip at the sneer forming on her beautiful soft pink lips. She mirrored my previous gesture and leaned in, her breath hot on my ear sent my nerves in an excited frenzy.

I loosened my grip as she whispered, "Never underestimate me."

I furrowed my eyebrow in confusion, and that was enough of an advantage for her. She pushed me away, loosening my hold on her and I stumbled backwards. She reeled her arm back – not losing any ground on the advantage she'd gain - and punched me square in the jaw. Pain shot up inside me, but only for a moment because my blood pumping and racing numbed me of the pain.

She huffed, turning on her heel and stomped away when I saw Gabriel entering. "What's going on here?" He asked.

Kimberly stormed past him and I answer, "She punched me. It was kind of hot."

She turned back and sent a deadly glare that could pierce any living creature including me, but I was more enthralled by the power she carried. She was a captivating creature herself. The doors banged close, reverberating a loud echo throughout the room.

Gabriel chuckled and I eyed him suspiciously. "What?"

"I knew it would happen sooner or later."

I scoffed. "She caught me off guard. It was a lucky hit."

"Sure, whatever helps you sleep at night."

I rolled my eyes. She had used her sexiness to diffuse my concentration. Try as I might I couldn't deny the attraction I held for her, which made me powerless and thus allowed her to get a lucky shot in. Everything I previously thought dissipated whenever she was near like she'd cast her own spell against me. What my mind wanted was being overpowered by what my heart yearned for. It was a battle raging inside of me and only one side could win.

At the moment, my heart was winning no matter how hard my mind tried to stop it.

CHAPTER 12

The next few days were agonizing as training commenced and we were ordered to stay in the safety of the grounds until further notice. From my knowledge no Keepers were dispatched to fight the evil creatures that roamed the earth, not even full fledge Keepers. It was absurd. We were just sitting here, taking no action while demons were out in the world causing havoc and killing innocent people.

It was infuriating being locked up like some kind of animal without being in its frequent habitat. I needed to get out, but like a tiger I was caged in with no plausible means of escape. It was maddening and there were times where I felt like I was going insane. It had been too long since I'd made a fresh kill. I needed to feel the release of all this pent of energy I carried inside of me and use it to rid the world of demons for the safety of humanity and time. On our routine training round, fighting with my fellow Keepers wasn't enough. No one was a match for my strength and agility other than Gabriel and we usually ended in a grid lock; neither winning nor losing.

If only I could sneak out and go fight a demon…then I could get my frustrations out on something rather than someone.

No. That wasn't even a possibility.

If I blatantly disregard their order I would get tracked the second they noticed I've escaped and bring me back to face the consequences. The Council would probably even strip my powers without a thought, leaving me weak and vulnerable temporarily until they saw fit. As much as I wanted to fight a demon and send it back to hell, it wasn't enough of a temptation to possibly lose my powers for my disobedience.

I just need to find something to occupy my time.

Reading turned out to be my distraction. After training was over for the day, Gabriel and would go to the library. We would sit there for hours, pouring over dozens of books trying to find any kind of record that resembled the events happening now. We spent four days, reading over ancient books that dated back to the seventh century. Most of the book's binding were falling apart and its pages withered with age. Translating wasn't the problem as we both knew Latin, Greek, and Hebrew. There was no language barrier when reading; the problem was finding nothing seemingly interesting.

"How can there be absolutely nothing about this? We both heard that this has happened before. Where are the records?" Gabriel asked, shutting the book he was reading.

"If it's a secret like our fathers told us then the records would be sealed. They wouldn't be so careless to leave it lying around in a book."

Gabriel ran a hand through his hair, frustration written all over his face. "This is useless. We won't find anything in these books. What is the big secret? What could have happened centuries ago to want the Council to hide a matter of urgency from us?"

I shook my head. "Don't know. Grabbing dinner might help. C'mon, we need to eat something to think on our feet."

He rubbed his temple, "Eating is the least of my concerns."

"Well, it's mine. We'll go see if anyone has found anything new. I doubt that we're the only ones trying to find answers."

Reluctantly, he stood up from his chair and headed for the door. I followed a few steps behind, letting him lose himself in his thoughts. I was concerned about his well-being. Ever since we've been back from Paris he's been distant, weary, and distracted. Not to mention that his skin was unnaturally pale and there were deeply etched dark circles around his eyes. There was something troubling him; thoughts that I wasn't privy to. He's completely shut me out, which makes me curious as to what he could possibly be thinking about.

Entering the dining hall we were greeted by novices and Keepers as they passed by chatting with friends or a tray of food in their hands. The hall was filled with novices, Keepers, and I even saw Elder Rocovik and Elder Marrino occupying a table in the far corner of the room. Laughter and chatter filled the hall with a low buzz, traveling to my ears in small audible waves.

I relished in the amount of freedom we've had the past few days but too much of a good thing was never good in the end. My sanity was in question with the amount of free time I've been allowed and it was becoming under rated being kept on the grounds. Training. Fighting and killing demons. It was the way of life that I'd become accustomed too, and taking two of

the factors out of the equation was testing my sanity – my way
of life.

Maybe, how I felt was what was troubling Gabriel. Surely, he
was also going off the edge being caged in like some kind of
animal. It was in our blood to seek, fight, and kill. It wasn't
good to keep us away from our nature for this long.

You're definitely going insane. What are you a predator?

I took a deep breath. I seriously needed to get a grip on reality
and calm down. There was no point in wishing in things I
wanted most. It never came to any good.

Gabriel and I grabbed a tray from the side of the buffet bar
and began to pile up our plates with deliciously made food
for the evening. We served ourselves a heaping of spaghetti
with spinach lettuce on the side. Gabriel doubled up on mash
potatoes and gravy, while I grabbed two pieces of barbecued
ribs. It all looked delicious and their heavenly aroma assailed
my nostrils. I licked my lips, savoring at the food in front of me.
I couldn't wait to dig in and replenish my growling stomach.
With our Coke in hand as our last addition for the first round,
we headed towards a table where I saw Beth, Nole, and Kimberly
eating.

"Mind if we join?" Gabriel asked.

"Hey guys!" Beth said turning around and scooting over to sit
closer to Nole, allowing us room to join. "Of course not! I was
actually waiting for you guys."

I raised my eyebrow and sat down in the chair next to Kimberly. She didn't look at me and instead was finding the plate
of strawberries in front of her rather interesting. I cast a side
glance at her and found that she was peeking through her long

blond hair at me, her eyes a piercing soft blue. I offered her a smile, but she quickly averted her eyes back to her plate of strawberries.

Kimberly was a lot of things – shy, being one of them. I found her cute when she would look the other way at me like a little girl who had a crush. She was also feisty, strong, sexy, and utterly enticing. Images of the fight we had a few nights ago surfaced in my mind – none lasting more than a few seconds. The way she looked at me before she made her move to attack brought a chill down my spine that both unnerved and thrilled me; the kind of look that sent my nerves on end at her tender and fiery gaze.

"This is really nice, Beth."

I snapped out of my thoughts once I heard Kimberly's soft voice. All my senses came crashing back at me and suddenly the room seemed too loud even to my ears, the lights too bright; everything was a bit disorienting.

"It's really good, actually." Kimberly said laced with astonishment. She gasped and I looked over to the admiration in her eyes. "How long did it take you to do this?"

There was a book in her hand and she flipped through the pages delicately as if it was a long ago treasure that needed to be cared for. I scooted my chair closer to her and saw that she was looking at pictures of us; pictures from our day in Paris. They were the pictures that Beth had taken and I distinctly remember her saying she was making something out of them. This must have been it.

Kimberly suddenly stopped at a page and began to laugh, her hand flying to her mouth to stifle the giggles that arose.

"What's so funny?" Beth asked, leaning over the table.

"This," she pointed at a picture of us and I cocked my head to the side to see what she meant. In neatly printed handwriting were the words Stupid Calder and a spiral pointing at the picture of Kimberly and I.

"Oh," Beth said, stifling the laugh on her lips. I crossed my arms over my chest and pushed the plate in front of me in mock hurt. Gabriel looked up and a small smile began to form from the corners of his mouth. But his eyes were still weary and lifeless.

"Aww, c'mon Cal! Stop pouting. You ruined the picture with not smiling and all."

"I'm not the only one in the picture."

"Yeah, but you were being an ass hence why I'm not too happy here," Kimberly pointed at the picture again and laughed. I couldn't help the smile that began to form on my lips. The picture was not one of my better ones. We looked miserable. It was the picture taken before we all went out to dinner. Kimberly and I were not on the best of terms and she wanted nothing to do with me.

I looked at the picture of us – the background was dark as if the lights had gone out only illuminating the both of us. That was virtually impossible because I remember that the lights did no such thing. Kimberly's face was drawn in a small frown; her eyes warm yet had the power to pierce right through my soul. I had a similar frown on my face while my hands were in my pockets, waiting for Beth to take the picture of us.

"I remember how poor Beth was deflated afterwards. I now see the reasoning for it." Nole said jesting.

I chuckled. After Kimberly finished leafing through the pages of the scrapbook she passed it to me. I the terrible amount of work Beth had put into this one book. It must have taken her days to complete. Her handwriting was written here and there more for her amusement like the 'Stupid Calder' scrawl. Some pages were filled with other people that she'd never met like the couple she took a picture of in front of the Concorde Bridge. I chuckled at the picture of Gabe near the Bridge, the expression on his face is priceless. He's totally caught off guard, his eyes unfocused and his cheeks red from the cold. There were also drawings of the bus we took in the morning we ventured out into Paris, a sketched Eiffel Tower, and the train we'd seen on our way to dinner.

Kimberly was right. This was good. I hadn't known that Beth was an artist and her sketches weren't awfully done. She had a gift. "Good job, kid." I said, handing the book back to her. "How long have you been drawing?"

"Not long. I'm not particularly good. I like doodling in the spare time that I have and we've been having a lot of that lately."

"Tell me about it." I took a drink of my Coke, resuming on eating my dinner. There was small chit chat around the table and I took comfort in the fact that Kimberly was done ignoring me after she had called me an ass earlier. If calling me an ass was all it took for her to forgive my recent behavior than I would take it with no questions asked.

A comfortable silence settled over us. We were all lost in our own thoughts as we ate. From across the table I saw Gabriel fiddling with the chain around his neck. It was blatantly obvious who he was thinking about. I focused my thoughts on his, but got absolutely nothing. He had put up a shield around his mind, making it hard to push through and read his thoughts. I had a feeling that if I did push then there would be dire consequences to pay. I'd probably be physically pushed out and have a raging headache for the next few days or worst – be cited for forcibly using my powers on another Keeper.

"I've been hearing things…" Beth said softly to Nole. I lifted my head, cocking my head to the side, concentrating on the words that had caught my attention. "It's something about a Keeper who was tortured by a demon long ago."

"Oh, the legend." Nole said gruffly. "Yes, it's a story about how a demon had captured one of us and tortured him until he gave it valuable information. Is that it?"

She shook her head, her eyes wide - urgent. "But there's more."

"Like what?" I asked. I leaned my elbows on the table, interested on what she'd heard.

Beth put down the spoonful of peaches she was about to eat, looking like she lost her appetite. "I heard his name was Parker. I heard some Keepers talking about it after training was over today. They said something about how someone else must have betrayed us in order for the demons to begin an uprising again."

I furrowed my eyebrows, taking in the information. Gabriel mirrored my concern and asked, "Are you sure this is what they said? Do you remember who they were?"

She shook her head, slowly. "I didn't see them. I stopped to tie my shoe and that's when I heard them talking about it. I hid behind a corner."

"You sure they didn't see you?" I pressed.

"Positive. I was out of there before either of them could know that I'd been listening." She cleared her throat, my eyes setting on the line of concern on her forehead. She fiddled with her fingers, locking her hands together one moment and the next unlocking them. Nole reached over and laid his hand over hers as a sort of comfort. "There's more that I heard other than the Keeper."

"Was is it?" Nole asked softly.

Beth's eyes traveled to mine then to Gabe's, and they finally rested on Kimberly's. Kim reached forward and held her hand saying, "It's okay. You can tell us. We won't say anything to anyone. It's between the five of us. Right guys?"

She turned to look at us, her eyes pleading for us to accept the promise. "Agreed." We mumbled.

Beth sighed, "I heard that there was also a war."

"This is all you heard, Beth, all of it?" Gabriel asked.

She nodded and breathed out a long sigh of relief. She leaned back in Nole's arms, her food forgotten replaced with lines of worry on her face. What if they found out I told...I might be kicked out of the Council or worst...have my powers revoked. Her emotions were radiating off of her in massive strings of concern. If they found out...I'd be labeled as traitor...what would they do? The looks on Gabe and Cal's faces mean that this information is important. If that's the case then I could be reprimanded for what I've shared...what if it's a secret and I've just uncovered it..?

I leaned forward, needing to let Beth know that her discovery was safe with us. "Don't fret, kid. We'll keep this between us. Okay? You don't need to worry."

She nestled her head in Nole's chest and I leaned back in my chair, thinking. There were two new elements that Beth had unearthed and it might very well be the secrets that my father said we'd come to learn once we came of age. The name of the Keeper was new information as was the war. The Keeper's name had been lost long ago, no one could even remember his name and so he was just called the "Keeper" when referred to the legend of the demon and him. Then there was a war. What war? I have never come across a war in my studies. Sure, there were battles that legendary Keepers had fought, but none involving a Parker or a war.

I caught Nole's eyes travel to mine and then to Gabriel's, assessing the gravity of the situation in our eyes. His eyes were hard, searching and unyielding – I found that I couldn't hold his gaze for too long before I had to look away from his unsettling gray gaze. "What is it? Is there a connection you two have gathered?"

"There might be." Gabriel said, pushing his chair back and taking his leave.

"Well, what is it?" Nole called out bur received no answer in return.

I remained in my seat, wondering where in the world he was going. The others faced me, looking at me for answers; answers that I did not have. But something was definitely wrong. The new revelations that Beth had delve us were indeed interesting and forthcoming.

The only connection I was able to make at the moment was that of the demon and the Keeper, Parker. What had he done...and what did Parker do to betray our kind? If it was the same story I heard back when I was a kid then Parker didn't do anything...he was just captured and tortured until the demon got what it wanted.

Shit.

The demon and the Keeper named Parker. Parker had been a traitor who had given valuable information about us to a demon... And the war that happened long ago was all connected. If Parker had betrayed us in giving the demon the secrets of our kind then it meant that a war would have happened. It made sense. It was a plausible conclusion. If that was true then it meant that it was all happening again...And if it was happening again it meant that we had a traitor in our midst.

Abruptly, I stood up, my chair screetching on the hardwood floor. "Calder, what's wrong?" Kimberly asked, worry laced in her voice. I needed to go find Gabriel. I needed to tell him what I'd figured out - maybe, it's the reason he ran out just few minutes ago.

"I have to go." I ran out of the dinning hall not caring of the set of eyes that were on me as I passed by. My heart was racing at this new development, needing to find Gabriel and tell him of the connection I made.

With my mind in a frenzy I didn't even realize that someone had followed me out of the dining hall, and was trailing behind me - keeping to the shadows.

Chapter 13

As I got closer to the library I felt someone following me; the hair on the back of my neck standing up. I whirled around peering into the torch lit corridor, but finding only the shadows of the fire as they danced on the walls. Uneasily I kept walking, listening intently to the sounds I made on the wooden floorboards.

I had been trying to get into Gabriel's mind to see where he was, but I was having no such luck. He had shut me out for reasons unbeknownst to me. Whatever he was hiding was affecting him in a way that I had never seen him act before. Not even the infamous Gwen Hampton could have this kind of negative effect on him.

Or maybe it was her...he's finally gone mad after all these years.

I heard the faintest sound of something drop behind me and I turned around to catch the sight of long hair disappearing around the corner. Backtracking, I saw a figure lurking behind the shadows of a column. As quietly as I could be I stepped closer only to hear the heavy still breathing of somebody.

Without giving it another thought I crept forward grasping the person's arm, pulling a surprised Kimberly from the shadows. I pinned her to the wall of the column, anger rearing its ugly head in my veins.

"What the hell are you doing?" I asked through clenched teeth.

She gulped, her eyes wide with fear only to turn into surprise that then turned into determination all in a matter of seconds; her eyes turning into a wide set of different shades before my eyes at her ever changing moods. "I want to know what's going on."

"This has nothing to do with you." I said, my voice clipped around the edges. I let her go, watching her closely, concentrating on reading her mind.

He's such an ass.

Well, that wasn't new. Calling me an ass seemed to be the perfect word to sum up my character. I scoffed, turning on my heel and continuing towards the library where I thought Gabriel might be. Unfortunately, getting rid of Kimberly served to be a different matter all together.

"If something is going on it concerns all of us, Calder, not just you and Gabe. You can't handle whatever the threat is by yourselves."

"We're not." I said, walking briskly but she was right there beside me – determination laced in her voice. I could practically fell the eager energy coming off of her in sonic waves, unrelenting and incalculable.

"Okay. Well, what's going on then? What was that Keeper story you guys were talking about and the demon and-"

I spun around pushing her against the wall, my body pressed to hers as my hand covered her mouth. "Not here." She nodded, her crystal blue eyes widening at my abruptness. I took in a deep breath, my nostrils filling with the scent of watermelon and something else - something that smelled vaguely like lilacs. My hand slowly fell to my side as I stared into her clear blue eyes. Curiosity flickered in them for a second before she dropped her gaze; a strand of hair falling into her eyes.

Fire ignited in my brain and traveled south. The want -no, the need was too impossible to ignore. I stepped back as a burning sensation formed within, making my breath labored. "I-I," I started but was unable to form coherent words. I cleared my throat, taking a few more steps away from her. "We need to go and find Gabriel. I'll tell you what's going on when I can."

"Okay," she said softly. "That's all that I was asking for."

No, I wanted to say. No, there was more that she wanted, but did not voice. It was the same thing that I found myself wanting like never before. There was a deep sense of longing settling itself in the middle of my chest with no sign of leaving any time soon. It had taken residence there and as much as I tried to deny it - I could not any longer.

Neither could she as I read her thoughts for the briefest of seconds.

"Gabriel, what in heaven's name are you doing?" Gretchen asked over my shoulder.

"Need to find a record." I muttered, dropping books to the floor in my haste.

"Gabriel! You need to be careful! They are ancient archives and you're treating them like they are nothing more than a sack of potatoes with-"

"Sorry." I turned around, giving her a sheepish smile. "I'll be careful, promise."

She eyed me warily over her glasses, not believing me at first, but finally resigning. "You better or I will have to tell your father about this, Gabriel."

I nodded and turned back to the shelf, quickly scanning over the titles on the bindings. I heard Gretchen's steps fade minutes after she was satisfied that I wouldn't mistreat her books. They weren't hers, but she treated them as a mother would her child. She tended to the ones that were ill-treated, mending their bindings to new; while the others were taken care of from becoming torn and dusted them frequently – like every day.

It wasn't in me to be acting this way, but I needed to find any sort of record of the Keeper named Parker, the demon, and a so-called war. From my knowledge I have never learned or even heard about a war. The only piece of the puzzle that was concrete was the legend of the Keeper and the demon. I remember that cold July night when I was a novice and the elder Keepers took us to the forest to train for the week. On our last night they told us our version of a scary story because being tortured by a demon to the point that self-generation did not work – was frightening.

It was a Keepers worst nightmare.

In the legend, Parker was tortured because the demon wanted information. The kind of information it wanted is unknown; lost in the sands of time. Then today we get new information

from a conversation Beth had heard, mentioning that the information the Keeper gave the demon caused a war - a war that is
not mention in any of our history books.

My theory consists of weaving the three subjects together to
form a plausible conclusion. First were the Keeper, Parker and
the demon. If the demon had captured Parker long ago to get
valuable information then it must have had succeeded in order
to begin a war. Parker must have delved secrets that pertained
to our world, giving the demon an advantage and thus striking
us at our most vulnerable.

Vulunerability was not something we let ourselves encounter
because of the danger it opposed to others. That's why we had
safety protocols, sacred rules, ect. to ensure our protection and
the security of others like humans.

I need a record to show when safety protocols increased, I
thought as my eyes searched and read the bindings of the books.

"Ah-ha!" I plucked the book from the shelf and blew the dust
of the cover, making me sneeze as the particles settled in the air
around me. The title was etched in gold handwriting reading
Proteggere I Consigli: Ragioni per le Quail, Come e Quando.
Protecting the Council: Reasons Why, How, and When – this is
exactly what I needed and was lucky to have come across it as I
see it wasn't in its rightful place.

Taking the book in hand I began to walk but stopped, feeling
a rush of vertigo settle upon me. I stumbled, feeling heavy when
I tried to walk. I righted myself on one of the chairs as the book
fell out of my hands with a loud thump. The room spun in my
eyes and I caught a glimpse of a golden light floating between
the book cases, illuminating the spot in warm light.

"Gabriel?"

Tearing my eyes away from the book case I looked down to see Gretchen's concerned eyes assessing me, her hand lightly resting on my forearm. "You should get some water. You look really pale. Have you eaten?"

I nodded, waving away her concern. There was nothing that she should worry about as the sudden wave of dizziness had subsided. "I'm fine. Sorry about the book."

The wrinkles at the corner of her eyes tightened as she smiled, making her eyes glow with amusement. "Don't worry about it, dear. Just slow down your endeavors." She ruffled my hair and was off again towards her desk.

I smiled. Gretchen had always treated me like her grandson. Actually, now that I think about it – Gretchen never had children of her own and treated us like the loving grandmother she would have been. It's one of the reasons that I stopped mistreating her books when she asked me to; I did not want to disrespect her wishes.

There was a sudden chill in the air and I shivered only to remember what I had seen while I was dizzy; in a haze of some sort. I glanced towards the book case where I had seen the light, but didn't see anything there now. It had been almost a week since I last saw the light/ghost. Since I'd seen it I felt like it had become part of me, calming and soothing at the right moments. But now without seeing its presence constantly was affecting me physically, at least that is what I thought. It was the only explanation I had for the drastic change in physic that has afflicted me.

Sighing, I crouched down to pick up the book and saw that it landed to an opened page. Picking up the book in my hands I read, Barriera Invisibile. That meant Invisible Barrier translated to English from Italian. My eyebrows furrowed, curiosity getting the best of me. It was an interesting page to have stumbled upon. I stood up, reading the contents of the page as I walked to a table.

La barriera dell'invisibilità è una nuova tattica rafforzate in l'inizio del xv secolo.

The invisibility barrier was a new tactic enforced in the early fifteenth century.

E' garantita la sicurezza dei Consigli in tutta Europa, mentre weilding magic per creare un solido campo invisibile intorno alla sede (vedi, 459).

It ensured the safety of the Councils throughout Europe, while wielding magic to create an invisible solid force field around the headquarter (see 459).

I mulled over what I had just read, taking in the information and storing it in a file for later. I always believed that the invisibility barrier was a safety protocol that was enacted since the beginning of time when the Councils were formed throughout Europe. From the text that I had just read it said that the barrier was formed in the early fifteenth century to ensure the safety of the Councils. Why would the Councils barely enact the invisibility barrier seven hundred years ago? There must be a reason why it was instituted at that time.

I looked back down at the page, almost forgetting that it was directing me to go to another page. I hurriedly flipped to page 459 only to find that there was no page. I flipped back and forth in frenzy, but page 459 did not exist. I turned back to page 458 and page 461 and saw that a page had been torn out of the binding. I ran my fingers through the crevice, feeling the jagged pieces of paper left behind. The work to hide the evidence had been gingerly done in a way that someone would not notice it at first glance.

Someone was trying to hide the continents of that page.

My stomach dropped as a deep knowing feeling settled in my bones. Whatever was written on page 459 was important and contained the knowledge we were seeking. It contained the why; why the invisibility barrier was enacted in the fifteenth century. I had a feeling that it was because of the demons – because of the war.

There had been an uprising- an uprising dictated by a demon. That's what the Council was hiding from us. That's what all the Councils were hiding from us because they didn't want any of us to know.

But why?

Why didn't they want us to know such a crucial part of our history?

"Gabriel!"

CHAPTER 14

I whirled around at the sound of my name only to find a frantic Calder and breathless Kimberly. Gretchen cleared her throat giving me a reprimanding look over her shoulder. I sent her my best apologetic smile for my friend's rude manners. She sighed, shaking her head in disapproval, and went back to tending to the books in front of her.

"Where have you been?" Calder asked through clenched teeth.

I raised my brow at the tightness in his voice. There was a wild look in his eyes and I cast an apprehensive look to Kimberly noting the redness in her cheeks. Slowly I said, "I've been here since I left the caf," I dropped my voice to a whisper and added, "I found something."

He raised an eyebrow and nodded – understanding the gravity of the situation. "Not here. We should go somewhere private."

I nodded in agreement. Grabbing the book from the table we headed out of the library and into the corridor where the torch lights lit on my command. I heard a small gasp of wonder from Kim, and I looked back to see her in awe. She was still fairly new to this new world. My guess was that she didn't know I wielded magic. It was part of me as much as I needed the air to fill my lungs to breathe. If I recall I don't think she's ever seen me use my power aside from casting a spell, but that was something we all could do a little of.

"So where are we going?" She asked softly, her voice traveling in the small space between us.

Calder and I exchange a knowing glance as a grin broke his face. "It's a secret."

"So now you know." I said, watching Kimberly intently as worry lines began to crease her forehead. She had stayed silent as Gabriel and I delved her in our theories and assumptions along with enlightening her about the Keeper Legend.

"Do you believe they are keeping all of this a secret to protect us?" She asked.

Gabriel took a seat for the first time since we entered our underground hideout beneath one of the gazebos. The old wooden chair creaked under his weight. Wearily, Gabe puts his head in his hands as exhaustion sets in his slacked form.

"The question is – why are they trying to protect us?"

Kimberly shook her head, not knowing what to say as her blue gaze traveled around the small room. I rubbed at my temples in small circles trying to rid the ache of all the information we have gathered today. Gabriel's theory was probable and it was more in depth than I ever would have thought. But in sharing my only assumption he agreed that there might be a traitor in our midst. It would be a significant factor if there truly was an uprising and what happened centuries ago was happening again as we spoke.

The last piece of the puzzle was why.

Why did the Councils mutually agree to hide a war from our history?

What was the purpose of that other than keeping it hidden for future generations?

What exactly happened?

"I'll see you guys tomorrow at training," Gabriel said, casting a look at his watch. "Have a goodnight."

"Night," Kimberly said as I slightly nodded in his departure. One moment he was there and then he was gone in an instant as he used a teleportation spell to leave rather than going up the ladder and through the gardens to the castle.

He had it easy.

"So what are we going to do about this?" She asked breaking the silence in the room. "Are you going to tell your father or Elder Montehue?"

I leaned my head back against the wall and closed my eyes. "They don't want us to know. We discussed what happened at the French Council with them, and they told us that whatever is happening is a secret reserved for when we become full fledge Keepers."

"But why," she muttered. "What is the point of keeping a matter of importance, such as this, a secret? Wouldn't they want us to learn of Parker's mistake so that we could prevent it from repeating?" She slumped down on the chair that Gabriel had occupied and propped her chin in her hands as her elbows rested on her knees. "It must have been dreadful what Parker went through if he broke the Vow of Secrecy. I couldn't even begin to imagine what the demon had done to him."

Her voice was full of sympathy as I listened intently, depicting the rise and fall of her breathing. She sounded distant, but I knew that she was just a few feet away from me – lost in her own thoughts as she tried to make sense of the information.

"We should follow Gabriel's example and head to bed," I said, not bothering to open my eyes as they would have fallen to her beautiful face. They would betray the emotions I was trying to silence deep within. Being alone with her was becoming dangerous as it ensued a burning desire like nothing I've ever felt before.

"You're right," I heard her get up from the chair and begin to climb the ladder. "You coming?"

"You go on ahead. I'll see you tomorrow."

"Okay," she said softly with a hint of sadness laced in that one word. Only when I heard the trapdoor clamor shut did I open my eyes and let out the breath I did not realize I was holding.

The next few days Kimberly, Gabriel, and I spent our time flipping through ancient texts in the library. Gretchen began to eye us suspiciously wanting to know what we were up to, but Gabriel managed to keep her curiosity hindered. There were always pieces of new information that we gathered, but they ended in dead ends just like the concept of the Barriera Invisibile. We were discovering that there were more missing pages as the days passed.

The Midnight Masked Ball was approaching with only three days to prepare. When we walked into the dining hall that evening we began to see the small details that commenced the transformation for the grand night. There were exquisite, sparkling lights hanging around the room as they illuminated the vast space. The grand double staircase that was on the other side of the room was draped with a deep plum carpet, giving the room a warm illusionary sense. The marble columns were brought out and on top sat brass light fixtures, basking the room in an amber glow.

"It's so beautiful!" Kimberly beamed. "I have to go get a dress."

"You haven't gone shopping yet?" Gabriel asked.

She shook her head. "We've been busy," she dropped her voice to a conspirator whisper, "'studying' that I haven't had the time."

"We should go tomorrow afternoon. We'll ask Beth and Nole if they'd like to come along." I suggested.

They shook their heads in agreement as I wondered who our chaperon would be to accompany us on our day out of the castle. We still were not allowed to leave the safety of the castles barrier, but with the ball approaching the Council had made an exception. We were only allowed to leave if we went in a group –there are safety in numbers – and if one of the Council Elder's accompanied the group.

"Hey, guys. Mind if I steal Kim away for a moment?"

I turned my head to see Lucas standing next to Kimberly, his hands stuffed in his pockets. I did a quick read of his mind, finding his intentions on the very surface of his thoughts. Gabriel raised his eyebrow – the scar becoming visible under the pristine lights. We shook our heads and I watched as he led her away towards the entrance of the hall. There was the fracture of a moment where everything and everyone fell into the background as I watched her walk away with him. She threw a glance over her shoulder as she found my eyes. Our gazes locked for a second before Lucas grabbed her hand, her attention turning to his.

"He's probably asking her to the ball," Gabriel said.

"He is," I confirmed.

Gabriel furrowed his eyebrows sending a strong telepathic message asking me: What are you doing? Go after her, you idiot.

What's the point? Lucas is better for her than I ever could be.

He shook his head, disappoint and annoyance written clearly on his face. He's not the one she wants, Cal. You are blind and foolish if you can't see that.

Without another thought he began to make his way towards our table where Beth and Nole greeted him. I stood there transfixed as an overwhelming sinking feeling settling at the very core of my being. Gabriel's words rang loud and relentlessly in my head until I took a step towards the entrance of the hall, clearing my head and making the pain in my stomach diffuse.

The next moment I was running out of the dining hall. Every step I took bringing me closer to her.

I was too late.

My feet came to a stop as I saw Lucas lean in and kiss Kimberly tenderly. I felt as everything around me came crashing down as I was swept away by the dangerous, looming waves of the sea. Anger followed shortly after as I clenched my fists, wanting to punch Lucas in the face - sending him reeling backwards. I clenched my jaw at the thought. It was irrational and I knew it. But it was how I felt. It was the very thing I was trying to prevent.

I ran farther down the dim filled corridor, away from the scene. My heart beat pounded loudly in my ears as I ran - with every step I took it grow increasingly loud until it thundered in my head, filling my mind with its ruthless tune.

I reached the end of the corridor, a dead end. Sinking down to the wooden floorboards, my body slacked in defeat. For the past few months I had buried my feelings for her, hiding the fact that I felt more for her than the other girl's I've dated and slept with. This was something more. She was something more. Kimberly made me feel something entirely new and foreign – something that I hadn't been seeking, but found unexpectedly.

I had ruined my chance with her because I had been foolish and cold-hearted, not seeing what I had in front of me, and taking it for granted. Was this what love did to someone? Did it take siege of a person's heart, making it a prisoner of its own desires? Was this what Gabriel and my father felt when they couldn't be with the person they loved? It was poison as intoxicating as it might be – painfully persistent.

"Cal?"

I stopped thinking as her voice broke through my thoughts. There was no guess to who the voice belonged to as I would recognize it from anywhere. Kimberly stepped out of the shadows, and I barely made out her profile. I did a quick spell to ignite the torches against the walls, filling the hall with light and warmth.

When I looked back at her the look on her tender face made my heart swell inside my chest with something that I could only guess as hope. She walked forward and slid down the wall to sit next to me. He breath caught in her throat as she said, "I saw you."

I was silent and leaned my head back against the wall, feeling her soft gaze burning through my soul. The thought of her seeing me run past made me a coward, and she pitied me. That's why she was here. It was in her nature to tend to wounded beings – isn't that what all girls did? She probably looked at me like a small defenseless kitten that'd just gotten stabbed through the heart. She just wanted to take care of me, and make sure I was well.

The next thing she did stopped my thoughts in their tracks – a fast moving train abruptly stopping as the engineer pulled the brakes. Kimberly grasped my hand, slowly lacing her fingers through mine. I glanced down at our joined hands and then looked into her soft blue eyes. There was no denying that this moment felt right, and I was done trying to bury my feelings deep within my core. There was no need to pity myself any longer, and I was done thinking that I didn't deserve her.

"I saw you and I know that you saw Lucas kiss me, but when he did all I could think about was you."

Her hand trembled in mine and I lifted our join hands to brush a kiss on her knuckles. She smiled and leaned in towards me until our foreheads touched and we looked into each other's eyes. She was beautiful in a way that I'd never seen anyone else before. She was different, seeing me for who I really was – breaking down the barrier I had carefully built with her infuriating and stunning nature.

"Your poison," she said. "Painfully sweet."

A small laugh escaped my lips. "Have you ever thought that's what you are to me?"

The corner of her mouth curved into a smile as she leaned in and closed the gap between us, her lips crushing into mine. The smell of watermelon filled the air between us in an enveloping aroma. The kiss was soft and nothing like what I had ever experienced. It was warm and sweet just as she was. It filled with the care and affection we had for one another. Her hand went up to touch the side of my cheek and I felt my body burn at her touch.

I deepened the kiss, lacing my hand in her hair as I pulled her closer to me, bringing her into my lap. The kiss grew feverish as all the burning desire we've been hiding surfaced between us. She nipped at my lower lip, and a small moan escaped from my lips in return. Sliding my hands to the back of her thighs I lifted her up in one swift motion as her legs wrapped around my waist in a vice. I pushed her up against the wall, trailing kisses from her ear to her neck. She moaned as I grabbed her wrists and pinned, them above her head with one hand as I pressed my body to hers.

There was no will to break free from my touch like that die in the training room where we fought, but instead she welcomed my hands as they dangerous slid down her body – heating up my body in a sensation that could only be brought when I was near her. Desperately, she broke free from my grasp and took my face in her hands as she lavished me with a fierce and burning kiss.

There was no one else in this frozen moment of time. It was just the two of us enveloped in the want – no, the need of our bodies, minds, and hearts. The moment I realized that there was something I needed to tell her - words that I'd never spoken to anyone before, she pulled away – pushing me back hastily, her small fist connecting with my chest.

I opened my eyes to see her wild and frantic blue eyes as she glanced around the corridor in a daze. "Kimberly?"

"I-I," she stammered. Her eyes were wide with fear as she blinked to get rid of the thoughts that seemed to be surfacing her minds. My breath was labored and I took deep calming breaths to regulate my breathing back to normal. The rushing of blood in my ears slowly faded, but I watched as Kimberly became anxious as the seconds passed. My eyebrows furrow in confusion at her sudden change of behavior. I took a step towards her, reaching out my hand but she recoiled. Shaking her head she said abruptly, "I have to go," and ran down the corridor.

She was gone before I could utter another word, leaving me confused at what had occurred between us. But as positive as the sun rises and sets, I was certain that I had found what I had been denying for months. There was no mistaking the feeling that burned at the tip of my tongue – the word that I never imagined in all my life existed. The very word that I'd said to be a curse as I'd seen the damage it could do firsthand. But in life there are always exceptions, contradicting everything a person once believed in.

Kimberly was mine.

CHAPTER 15

K imberly

I ran as fast as I could away from Calder, my legs and chest burning with exertion. When I got to my room I hastily shut the door behind me and began to pack. Leaving Calder hurt more than I could ever have explained. He'd finally kissed me and it was all that I had ever wanted since the day of our mission together. He was stubborn and infuriating, but behind his cold demeanor there was more to him. There always had been.

But I had to leave him as fast as I could once I got the message from my brother, Nick. He was in trouble and he wouldn't have called me, vividly giving me a message of his whereabouts if it wasn't of dire importance. If I had stayed any longer with Cal he would have read my mind and seen what I was receiving. As soon as he put the information together, Calder would have stopped me from going to aid my brothers. The next thing he would have done was go to the Council and informed them of the situation. The Council then would contact the Russian Council – giving the matter to them since it was Nick and

Halston's home base. It would be a never ending process! They would do everything with consideration and precision, wasting away precious time to dispatch Keepers to them.

Time was a luxury my brothers did not have. I would go alone and try to help Nick and Halston the best I could. They were in trouble and I was the only one who could help them. I was the only one who knew where they were.

A knock at the door disturbed my frenzied packing. Quickly, I hid my brown leather messenger bag under the bed from prying eyes. To my utter shock it was Lucas when I opened the door. Disappointment filled my heart, softly tugging on its edges. There was a small part of me that had hoped Calder would be the one at the door, wanting an explanation for my abrupt departure.

Lucas stood in the doorway, his hands stuffed in his pockets. There was dejection written all over his light green eyes, sending a jolt of guilt through my body. "What are you doing here?" I asked.

"I wanted to come by and talk about earlier," he said sheepishly. "Can I come in?"

"No," He looked at me apprehensively, trying to read the expression on my face to give him any sort of indication of what I was thinking. Lucky for me, he wasn't Calder and couldn't know in an instant what I was doing or thinking.

"I was just heading to bed. It's late," I said, hoping that he would leave. It was late and I needed to get to my brothers before something worst happened.

He crossed his arms over his shoulders, a sign that I knew all too well. He wasn't leaving and I sighed in resignation. I stepped to the side, letting him walk into my room as he took a seat on the edge of my bed.

I closed the door behind me silently and made my way to the window seat, catching my reflection in the glass. A small gasp of incredulity escaped my lips. My hair was in disarray and my lips were red, swollen by Calder's desperate kisses. I racked my hand through my hair smoothing it out as best I could. There was nothing that I could do about my mouth. They would heal in a bit. The ability to self-generate was in my blood, and the moment I realized that I began to see the red puffiness of my mouth lessen before my eyes.

I turned around to face Lucas' downcast eyes as he idly played with his hands in front of him. A tremor of pain grasped my heart at his saddened lopsided smile. It broke my heart to see how much my rejection was affecting him. He was a great guy and a tremendous friend at that. He was the only one who I'd confessed my feelings for Calder to as he listened intently and patiently – pouring out the contents of my heart's desires.

Part of me knew how Lucas felt about me, but as I'd hoped nothing in our friendship changed when I admitted my feelings for Cal.

Well, that is until tonight.

When Lucas kissed me it was unexpected and I quickly broke away when I heard footsteps in the corridor, fading rapidly down the hall. Something in my gut told me that it had been Calder who had stumbled upon seeing Lucas and I, and he ran away from the scene. I followed after him, leaving a broken-hearted Lucas behind. I just couldn't stay with him, knowing that my heart was somewhere else in the depth of the shadows. If that wasn't enough of a reason to walk away from my friend then the image of Calder burning in my mind's eye made it clear when Lucas kissed me.

But everything changed tonight between Lucas and me. The kiss was the reason why the atmosphere in the room was awkward when before I could completely be myself around him. Now, it was filled with uncertainty and regret.

Lucas cleared his throat, penetrating the silence of the room. I looked up, my thoughts fading as I saw the internal battle brewing behind his tender green eyes. "I wanted to apologize for-"

"No," my voice was soft as it cut his apology short. "There's no need to explain, Lucas. I'm not angry. I should be the one apologizing."

He furrowed his eyebrows together as confusion washed over his features. The small freckles on his cheeks made him look like a little kid who'd just been told that the sky wasn't blue; absolutely lost and feigning to understand. I grabbed the end of my hair and started playing with the tips as I tried to find the right words to say to him.

Lucas was still my friend despite what had occurred. I couldn't let that kiss between us ruin our friendship. He meant more to me than a kiss. I only hoped that he could forgive me because I didn't want to lose him as a friend. It was dangerous still caring for Lucas, while Calder and I had - well I don't exactly know where our relationship stood or if I could even call it that. I just knew that he wouldn't be too happy if he walked in and found Lucas in my room. Cal was threatened by Lucas from the very moment that I met him. At one point I let him believe that there was something more going on with Lucas and me because I liked seeing the jealousy in his eyes.

Horrible, right?

But in my defense I neither concurred nor denied his assumptions.

That was worth something, right?

"There's someone out there for you," I said. But as soon as those words had come out of my mouth I knew they rang true. They felt right like an electrical current surging through a light bulb. "We all have that person who is our other half, Luc. I know you'll find her."

He laughed but it didn't ring true – it felt forced. He raked a hand through his hair as he said softly, "Do you think I'm an idiot to have thought it was you?"

I stood from my seat and kneeled in front of him, taking his hands in mine. "We all feel like we've loved once in our lives," I said. I remembered the first time I thought I was in love with my next door neighbor. I was fifteen and thought that he was my whole world.

He wasn't.

"But in the future," I continued. "We realized that it wasn't love at all when we meet the one that is made for us. When you find her it will feel like nothing you've ever felt before and the feeling will make your heart quicken inside your chest. It's undeniable and familiar like the sense of exhilaration when you run. It takes the air out of your lungs, and makes your breath catch in your throat."

He smiled, his eyes lighting up with a glimmer of hope and mischief. "When did you get so poetic?"

I laughed, feeling the tension between us dissipating. "So, still friends?" I asked, tentatively.

He pushed himself of the bed and stood up, enveloping me in a hug. "Always." His voice was surprisingly light, and I relaxed in his arms – silently being thankful for his understanding. "I'll see you tomorrow at training."

No, you won't, I thought guiltily. But instead I said, "Of course. I'll be showing you up in combat," I teased, amazed at how easily the lie slipped from my tongue.

He chuckled. "We'll see. Have a goodnight," he said shutting the door behind him.

I counted to twenty before I began to gather my belongings once again. I checked the contents of my bag to make sure that I had everything I needed. Lastly, I grabbed my spell book and flipped through the pages to find the transportation spell. It would take a lot of energy and the only semblance of magic that ran through my veins. The spell needed to take me directly to my brothers or else I'd end up somewhere foreign and alone.

If I was a magic wielder like Gabriel this wouldn't even be a problem. But I had to make do with my gift. It would help my brothers defeat the raid of demons they'd encounter. These last few months I've gotten stronger and could control my telekinesis better than I had in the beginning. It wasn't much but it would suffice.

Halston had been poisoned by a Snipcriz demon, leaving Nick to fight the horde of the evil creatures by himself. They were lying low now, somewhere in England. I could only depict a sign that read Rococo Gardens in the shadows of the night.

Finally finding the spell, I closed my eyes and concentrated on my breathing, making it slow and even. My heart was pounding loud inside my chest as I let all my concerns dissolve into the back of my mind. After a few seconds, I began to feel the slow rush of magic flowing through my body - down to the tips of my fingers, giving off a tingly sensation. The air around me shifted as I felt a breeze caress my skin and the enticing aroma of flowers met my nose. I knew in an instant - without opening my eyes that I was no longer in the comfort of my bedroom.

CHAPTER 16

C alder

For purposes unknown the Council ordered that training be suspended until the end of the holidays. Gabriel and I thought that it was strange, but didn't question the order. It gave Gabriel and I more time to look over texts in the library.

The only thing missing was Kimberly.

"Stop wallowing," Gabriel said shutting the book he was reading and placing it in the "useless" pile. "You'll see her in an hour. We're still going to pick out our tux for tomorrow night."

"What makes you think I was thinking of her?"

He chuckled, his laughter echoing along the book cased walls. It was thunderous in the way that I imagined the book cases toppling over as books fell on the wooden floorboards in a clutter. I turned around to find Gretchen smiling instead of having an annoyed expression on her face for his volume. A quick read of her mind told me that she knew – she knew.

"How does-"

"It's not that hard to figure out," Gabriel said answering the question on the tip of my tongue. "Your character has changed."

I furrowed my eyebrows in confusion. "There's a different bounce to your step."

What?

You're in love, Gabriel thought. It was clear and strong enough to send me reeling. How did he know? No, better question: How did everyone know?

"I told you – you're acting different."

I closed the book I was working on reading in Greek and looked at him, curiously. "Can you read minds now? When did this occur?"

He chuckled again, finding the topic of conversation amusing. "It's not hard to read the expression written all over your face, mate."

"Things change," I said softly – reflecting on how drastically my way of thinking had changed once I began to consider my feelings for Kimberly.

Gabriel stood up, pushing his chair back in the process as he began to take some books in his hands to reshelf. When he came back there was a glazed look in his eyes. I knew that look all too well. He was thinking about Gwen and I suddenly understood the way he must have felt missing the one girl he's ever loved.

The feeling alone would destroy me. But I realized now that it's better to have known and felt love than to never have experienced it all. Life truly feels empty when love is out of the equation. I've never felt more alive than I do now – in this very instant as if the world were brighter, full of colors and smells that I've never quite seen or smelled before. It was exhilarating, simply for the fact that it was unknown territory, and the notion of discovering new land each day was riveting.

"Whatever you do, don't let her go so easily."

I looked up and saw the guilt and remorse on my best friend's face. The one thing he regretted most in his life was walking away from Gwen without saying goodbye and fighting for the right to do so.

Standing up, I went around the table and clasped a hand on my best friend's shoulder – letting him know in that small gesture that I now understood what Gwen meant to him. My voice was certain but light when I said, "Wasn't planning on it."

We were waiting for Nole, Beth, and Kimberly to show up for our rendezvous afternoon in the council chamber. The Council had decided that my father would be the one to accompany us as our escort. I had a feeling that he was coming for the sole purpose of speaking to me. The last time we talked had been three weeks ago and it hadn't ended on a good note. Ever since then I had avoided him and the "talk" he had threatened. It was time to put the past behind us and start anew and those were my intentions if we did talk during our brief time out of the castle walls.

The chamber doors opened and I turned around expecting to see the others arrive, but instead Mr. Amato entered disheveled and short of breath with Lucas in tow looking anxious. Something was wrong by the looks of horror on their faces.

"Amato, what is your concern?" Elder Montehue asked. "You look like you've seen a-"

"My daughter...she's gone," he said distraught.

"What?"

Everyone in the room turned their eyes to me as I felt the weight of their scrutiny burning through me. The word was out of my mouth before I could remember my manners. Kimberly was gone? I caught Lucas' stare and read his mind in an instant. He didn't even try to conceal his thoughts as they unraveled right before my eyes.

"You were with her last night." I said, my voice sounding accusingly. I stepped forward, anger boiling through my veins as I met his cold green eyes. "You were with her and you didn't even notice how she was acting?"

"I could say the same about you."

I seethed in anger as I stared into his face – at his clenched jaw and the fire dancing in his bright green eyes as he thought of ways he could hurt me. The thoughts didn't veer far from my own mindset. My gaze trailed down his arms to his tight fists as he contained the anger within. I went deeper into his thoughts trying to find any sort of indication in his mind about Kimberly's whereabouts, but came up empty handed. He didn't know anything.

There was one thing we both shared: guilt.

We should have known her intentions. I should have known after the way she left me last night. Something occurred when we were kissing and it caused her to leave immediately. Had she seen something or someone? Was that the reason she had run away? If that was the case then how was it even possible? That's not her gift...unless...

"What do you know?" Mr. Amato asked, snapping me out of my reverie. His eyes were questioning as he looked at Lucas and me in turn.

When his question was met with silence he yelled, "Answer me!"

"They don't know anything, Richard." Mr. Amato turned around to look at my father uneasily as his eyes still flickered to Lucas and I. "I just sense guilt because they should have known. Am I right?" He raised an eyebrow expecting an answer. We both slightly nodded our heads. It was enough.

"Have you contacted your sons?" Elder Montehue asked. "Maybe they could provide assistance in-"

"No, they are unavailable at the moment." He said exasperated. "Last I heard of them was before they set out for a mission in Britain. The Council there asked the Russian Council if they could be of-" he stopped mid-thought, remembering that there were others in the room.

"I see," was all Elder Montehue said. He glanced at both sides where the other members sat and they all exchanged a brief look with one another.

There's something going on, Gabriel's thought rang loudly in my mind – reverberating along the walls of my head.

Yes. There is and I feel as if I...

An image began to flicker in my eyes – like a movie where I was the only member of the audience. There were two men in the dark open space, dirt and blood staining their clothes. One of them had messy blond hair that was coated with dried blood from the massive gash on the side of his head. He was shivering in the coldness of the cave despite our body's natural way of adapting to a certain temperature.

Yes, it was a cave as the image became clearer behind my eyes. I saw the natural curve of enclosed walls as the cave expanded in other directions, giving the effect of a maze. The other boy started a fire in the corner, illuminating the vast darkness. Their shadows danced among the walls from the newly built fire, making their features clearer. The boy who built the fire had raven black in great contrast to the first, but his eyes were a startling blue that reminded me of one other person's.

Kimberly.

The cave and its inhabitants faded as a new image appeared in my mind, only lasting for a second before Gabriel's eyes blurred in my line of vision. The sound of voices slowly filled my ears as conversation commenced around me. The only person who had paid any notice of me was Gabe as his eyes searched mine for answers.

We have to go, I said telepathically to Gabe -the urgency in my words evident. I know where she is.

Gabriel turned away from me, crossing his arms over his chest and waiting for a break in the conversation between Amato in the Elders. I looked around the room and saw for the first time that Keepers had been called and were standing erect in the back in their corresponding ranks, watching the room before them with silent observance.

"Father?" Gabriel said clearing his throat. Everyone's eyes turned to him waiting for him to continue. "May we take our leave?"

Elder Montehue furrowed his eyebrows and idly waved us off as an afterthought. We bowed and hastily retreated out of the chamber. Once the chamber doors closed behind us we took off in a sprint towards the winding corridors. I briefly informed

Gabriel on the images I saw and sent him a clear image of the sign Rococo Gardens.

We halted near the north wing where no one was around, and quickly began to chant the words to the teleportation. The air around us began to shift as the magic ebbed from our bodies, filling the space around us as it transported us to our desired location.

Gabriel

We ran through the streets of London, our steps pounding on the cobblestones. We weaved through the clusters of teenagers as some shot strange looks our way. The audible whispers of conversation reached my ears, filling my mind with curiosity and awe. Calder and I were running at full speed and captured unwanted attention of the kids all around us.

"We need to stop."

He shot me an impatient look. "We don't have time to stop."

I clasped my hand on his shoulder and he halted, clenching his jaw. "People are staring. We're drawing attention to ourselves. We need to slow down."

He sighed in frustration but in the end he agreed. We continued in a brisk walk down the street until we came upon a wide expanse of greenery and the sign Rococo Gardens greeted us. We barely made it pass the entrance when I sensed something different in the air. I stopped in my tracks and looked around the garden only to find two teenagers who were around our age sitting on an old rusted bench.

The girl had long flowing chestnut brown hair, while the boy's head was covered in unruly blond locks. They seemed like a normal couple of kids on the surface. What had made me stop wasn't their presence, but the hot coppery stench that demons carried covered them both - mixing with the smell of violets near them. It was impossible to disregard.

"Cal?" I asked, my hand impulsively grazing the handle of my dagger in my jacket. "Can you get a read on him?" There was something off about him, but I couldn't pin-point exactly what it was. He turned, casting a glance our way and exchanged a few words with the girl. Whatever he had said made her move closer to him.

"No," Calder said as his brows furrowed in confusion. "But he might just be a human who has a gift. It would explain why he can block me and the stench you smell. They might be Hunters or had narrowly escaped an attack."

I wasn't convinced. There was more to them than meets the eye – Hunters or not. I was certain of it. "What about the girl?"

Calder fixed his eyes on her and got a read in a matter of seconds. He snorted.

"What?"

"She's comparing me to her boyfriend. I'm better looking, right?"

I rolled my eyes. Leave it to Cal to make a universal assessment that trivial in the midst of emergency. "Do you really want me to answer that?"

He shrugged and we took off at a run, leaving behind the odd sensation that I received from the couple.

Calder

I received another image of Kimberly's whereabouts that lead us towards an underground entrance at the center of the gardens. Her thoughts and memories began to mend with my vision until they became one. I couldn't distinctly separate what my eyes saw in front of me in the present from her past and present memories. A bond had formed between us and it was heightened by the gravity of the situation. It was like she was calling out to me with all her will, making it hard to ignore her pleas. I saw everything that she saw and felt; her care for her brother that was injured as she tended to his wounds; the hardness of the cold earth beneath her; the sound of approaching footsteps on the ground.

Kimberly and her brother with the raven colored hair stood up in a rush – weapons in hand as they saw the first Snipcriz demon crawl out of the shadows; its pinchers dripping with poison, and its eight black eyes solely on the two of them.

CHAPTER 17

"The demons have found them," I said in a rush. "There is just one from the last image I saw. But there must be more."

Gabriel nodded as we ran to find the latch that opened to the secretive underground cave. We found it hidden beneath a discreetly covered patch of tulips that was seamlessly made for its purpose. Gabriel and I would have never stumbled upon it if it wasn't for Kimberly's memories.

The hidden trapdoor opened with a creek, pitch darkness meeting our eyes as we descended down the ancient ladder. Once we reached the bottom of the cave Gabriel materialized a torch and set it ablaze, the fire illuminating our surroundings. It wasn't even a full minute that we were below that we heard the distant clattering of metal and grunting.

We ran in the direction of the commotion, unsheathing our concealed daggers. What we came to face was going to require more arsenal than our measly daggers. Gabriel must have thought the same thing as he materialized his sword in hand and tossed an extra to me. We engaged in the battle with the beastly Snipcriz demons, carefully minding their pinchers. They carried poison that would take days to heal from, not to mention the agonizing pain that ensued from the bite itself.

Snipcriz demon's were huge genetically altered spiders like a science experiment gone wrong. On a scale of 1 to 10 on the deadliest demon scale they were a 10 and could kill us if they released enough of their poison into our system.

When the demons saw two new threats they scattered away from Kimberly and Nick (I believe that was the dark haired brother's name), leaving only one demon for Kimberly to fight while Nick tried to manage with two. That left one demon for both Gabriel and I.

"How did you-" I heard Kimberly say, stopping mid sentence. A momentary look in her direction made my heart stop in my throat. She was lying on the ground, crawling away from the demon's advancement.

"Dammit!"

Feeling the anger from the demon in front of me and the fear for Kimberly's life, I stalked forward and dodged to the left as its pinchers made a move to penetrate my skin. But I was faster and I thrust my sword into its center, killing the disgusting creature.

When I turned around, I saw Gabriel finishing off his Snipcriz. He didn't waste time as he ran to the other side of the cave where Nick was still in the defense, fending off the two Snipcriz. I ran to my right where Kimberly was also on the defense, dodging the Snipcriz's pinchers as it thrust forward in swift moments, trying to bite her.

It succeeded.

Everything happened in slow motion as I saw it bite at her side, hooking its razor sharp claws into her head and releasing its deadly poison. Her agonizing scream struck a chord deep within my soul. Everything faded into the background and only the sound of her pain resonated within the chambers of my being. Boiling, hot rage consumed my every thought as I thrust my sword into the unsuspecting demon, and everything around me came rushing back in double time.

I sank down into my knees and curled Kimberly into my lap. A soft whimper of pain escaped her lips and I soothingly rocked her in my arms, feeling as if the world was crumbling around me. Gabriel and Nick were still in a fiercely tight battle with the other demons until Nick slayed his followed by Gabriel's defeat.

"How did you know I was here," she said breathlessly.

Her eyes were glazed over and I knew that her vision was failing her. She closed her eyes and said slowly, "I'm dying...I can feel it. Please, don't go."

"Shh...you're going to be okay," I said but even as I said those words a tremor of fear of their uncertainty hit me in full force. I didn't know how much poison the demon had inflicted into her system. We needed to get her back to the Council.

I stood, carrying her in my arms. She grabbed my shirt, clutching the material in her hand. "If I tell you," her voice trembled. She was determined to keep on speaking no matter how difficult it proved. "I love you," she whispered. Her eyes slowly closed, and her hold on my shirt loosened. "I love you, Calder Montgomery."

Her last words echoed around me in a vice before she slumped into my arms, teetering on the brink of the dark abyss.

"You deliberately disregarded our order!" Elder Montehue's voice boomed along the chamber walls. Gabriel and I both stiffened under his hard penetrating gaze. "What were you two thinking going out and handling the matter on your own? We could have prevented Kimberly's wounds if you all had come to us with the knowledge you obtained. We should strip all three of your powers temporary for blatantly disobeying orders!"

"We didn't want to waste time informing you with what we knew," I said through clenched teeth. I hated feeling like I was a little kid getting reprimanded for my actions, which is exactly what they were doing. The other council members were silently observing our father's undermining display.

My father scoffed, "That's not a particularly good reason."

"Agreed," Mr. Montehue added.

Gabriel crossed his arms over his chest, standing his ground. There was a stormy look in his eyes as he said, "We aren't the only ones who hid something of dire importance."

I saw the expression of alert cross all of the council member's faces. They stiffened – some tugging at the end of their black clad robes, while others clearly tightened their jaw and looked down at their hands. Their demeanor was enough to indicate that they were in fact hiding something. It was time to delve them with what we knew no matter the cost it brought.

"We know about the war and the Keeper who betrayed us," I began.

"We've gathered that it's happening again. That there is a demon causing all the recent demonic activity, but we don't know why you'd keep this kind of knowledge hidden from all of us."

My father opened his mouth to respond, but then closed it - uncertainty creasing his forehead. He looked over at Mr. Montehue. A silent conversation was exchanged between them, ending with Mr. Montehue slowly shaking his head.

"They have the right to know," Marrino said, speaking up for the first time. The other council members nodded in agreement as they stood up to leave.

Gabriel and I watched in confusion as McNolie was the last one to exit the chamber. The only members who remained in their seats were our fathers as resignation was palpable on both their faces. They stood up from their chairs and came forward to sit down on the steps in front of the dais. My father motioned for us to do the same, and I couldn't help the feeling of nostalgia wistfully circling deep within my chest.

"This secret is kept until all of you come of age and go through the rite to become a full-fledged Keeper," my father began. "But we should have known that the both of you wouldn't stop until you figured it out. We should have known that both of you were close to the truth when Gretchen notified us of your persistent studying."

I smile crept up on my lips. My father patted my knee and glanced at Mr. Montehue. "It began in the mid thirteenth century..."

Kimberly was sleeping soundlessly in the comfort of her own bed. Dr. Corvaul had deemed both her brother, Halston and Kim fully capable of recovering on their own. It would just take time. For now, I was just sitting on a chair beside her bed - waiting for the moment when she opened her eyes.

I watched as the moon circled the sky, slowly disappearing over the other side of the castle as the minutes turned to hours. The first few hours that I was here I thought about what Mr. Montehue and my father told us. It had cleared any confusion between our theories, which were correct as we came to the full knowledge of what had occurred centuries before.

Parker had indeed betrayed our kind by divulging secret information that was only privy to our world. The demon wanted that information to make his move and begin an uprising. Once he gathered what he needed he began to form an army of various demons to follow him. This was a part of the story when Gabriel and I asked a question to make sense of the story. We've always believed that demon's didn't have a mind to think logically. It wasn't in their nature. But we found out another secret that we would have gained once we went through the rite.

Demons could look like humans.

The reason that we're kept this valuable piece of information was because the Councils didn't want us to grow up believing that all humans could be potential demons. They would rather keep us ignorant than have us grow paranoid and learn to keep our guard around all humans.

The demon who began the uprising leads a war that lasted a century. At first, the Councils didn't know what was going on with the frantic demonic activity. Five years after the war began they discovered of Parker's treason when his body was found on the steps of the Greek Council in Greece, his home base. The pieces of the puzzle began to emerge when the demon called Levine showed himself with his army as they dropped off Parker.

That's when the bloodbath and the demon hunt began. It wasn't until the end of the thirteenth century that they found Levine and killed him, disbanding his army. Without a leader the demons couldn't act by themselves and thus, receded into a life of solitude as before. It was after the war that the Councils began to work on a security system like the Barriera Invisibile.

Parker had betrayed us by giving the demon knowledge of our secret passage ways, hidden tunnels, and revealing the inner-workings of our world. He also gave Levine the knowledge that we could only be killed by decapitation or an overly amount of poison injected into our body by a demon.

Before the war our number of casualties had been low, but with the secret of our death in the hands of demons it made it easier for them to kill us off.

No one ever found out the grounds for Parker's betrayal other than the desire to make the demon stop torturing him. There was a part of me that believed there was more reason than torture itself. We were loyal to our kind and to the sacred duty we'd been blessed with – so why betray that sacred bond?

When my mind remained circling around the same thought I decided to pick a book off of Kimberly's bookshelf and began to read. I chose a dog eared copy of Pride & Prejudice. It was fairly interesting and thought that Mr. Darcy's demeanor towards Elizabeth Bennet was just a ruse to hide his attraction for the girl.

It was ironic.

It was past midnight when she began to stir.

I closed the book I'd been reading in the dim lighting, and held my breath not wanting to wake her - unless it was by her own volition. Slowly, her eyelids fluttered open. Her blue gaze focused on my face as the fogginess that clouded her mind subsided. I heaved a sigh of relief when she smiled. I set the book down on the nightstand, reaching forward to caress her face in my hands.

"Did we kill them all?" She asked.

I couldn't help but let a small laugh escape my lips. "You've been unconscious for more than ten hours and that's the first thing you ask?"

She laughed but the action made her cringe. Her hand flew to the side that had been wounded and now was bandaged to contain and manage the injury.

"Is Hal okay?"

I nodded. "Yes, he's staying in one of our guest chambers with Nick." Taking her hand in mine, I said reassuringly, "We're all safe and we defeated them – to answer your first question."

"That's all I wanted to know...wait. There's more I want to know," she began to sit up, but the act proved to be difficult in her fragile condition.

I helped her sit up as cautiously as I could, not wanting to cause her any more pain than necessary. "What's your question?"

"How did you know where to find me?"

"That's easy," I said, leaning over to kiss the frown creasing her forehead. "I saw it. Just like how you saw your brothers were in trouble. Nick has the same gift as I do, right?"

She nodded.

"You were subconsciously sending me images of where you were. Or..." I gulped, debating on whether I should tell her my theory or if I should leave it alone. I chose the former. There was no use in lying to her about this. She bit her lip, waiting for me to continue. "Or we formed a strong bond. It would be the only other reason I could think of to-"

"It's that one." She said, smiling. "My brothers and I have a strong bond and it was the reason why I was the only one who could help." She sighed and began to rub small circles with the bad of her thumb on my palm. "Our dad wasn't around for most of Nick's life when he acquired his gift. He went off to the Russian Council the day after he found out he had telepathy.

"I was barely four when he left. When I was nine and Hal was thirteen, he gained his gift of telekinesis. It wasn't long after when I found out who my family really was and what I would become. When I turned fourteen, I began to get worried because Hal and Nick both gained their gifts at the age of thirteen. As the years passed and there was still no sign of my gift, I was sent to Milan – away from my family. But my brothers and I kept in close contact.

"Nick would frequently send me images of his training sessions with Halston. It was practice for him and its how our bond grew.'"

She stopped, turning her eyes to me. I had been quietly listening to her family history – storing all her story for future reference. I wanted to know her and I knew that I could have spent hours listening to her speak about the color of the sky or what she thought about the Pope. It wouldn't have mattered as long as I was with her.

Her lips parted as she softly said, "Our bond...I don't know how it was created, though. It's only been a few months that we've known each other and with Nick it took years."

There was one reason I believed our bond had formed so quickly – just one. I brought her hand up to my lips and softly pressed a kiss on her knuckles. When I looked up, I saw the slight blush that stained her cheeks.

"Love," I said the word softly and saw her eyes widened in disbelief. "It's because of our love. I love you Kimberly. You're my only one."

She unclasped her hand in mine to gingerly lay it on the side of my cheek. Her eyes were soft and filled with a deep and unconditional affection that it caused my heart to race inside my chest. She leaned forward as did I until our foreheads touched.

"I believe you, Cal." Her breath sent a shiver down my spine. I closed the space between us with a kiss, letting my will power crumble to smithereens. She smiled finally saying the words I'd long to hear again since this afternoon, "I love you too."

CHAPTER 18

Gabriel

Looking at my reflection in the mirror, I saw the remorse and guilt I could never leave behind. There were days where my longing for Gwen was too much to bear to the point where I was in the middle of erupting volcanoes – my feet rendered to their place with paralyzing intensity, incapable of halting the impending disaster.

Today didn't only symbolize the day where we received our sacred blessing. Today marked the day I saved Gwen from getting hit by the car that would have ended her life. But it wasn't the act itself that mattered, although it was important. What happened afterwards was a memory that I would never forget.

Her parents were out of town that night, and I had promised her I wouldn't say a word about the afternoon's events. She didn't want them to rush back home for her convenience so instead I stayed with her that night. We built a fire in her living room, the heat of the hearth warming our bodies. That night we cooked s'mores in the fireplace as we watched If Only on abcfamily. It was one of her favorite movies and I thought it was ironic to have this movie airing on the same night that I had saved her life.

It was in that moment that I realized my life would feel empty if I had lost her. If I had been a fragment of a second too late or if I never had been blessed with the gift of time then I would have lost the most important person in my life.

It was then that I first realized I was in love with my best friend.

"Gabriel!"

I snapped out of my thoughts and turned to a concerned Calder. "You alright, mate? I've been calling your name for the last five minutes. What's on your mind?"

My eyes looked over his tailored black suit and settled on the black-silver striped mask in his hands. I knew that I had forgotten something when I went to buy my suit this morning. "You don't happen to have an extra mask? I seem to have forgotten the small detail."

Calder took a seat on the edge of my bed and said, "No. But you can always make one appear out of thin air." He fiddled with the mask in his hands adding, "Don't change the subject."

I chuckled, turning back around to face the mirror – resuming on tying the silk black tie around my white collar. "There's nothing to talk about," I made the mistake to look at Cal's reflection in the corner and saw his brows raised. "Besides there are more important things to discuss – how's Kimberly?"

A grin broke his face – momentarily forgetting his questioning. His gray-blue eyes gleamed under the low light as he said, "She's healing quickly. Dr. Corvaul says that he's never seen anything like it before. She should be recovering through Christmas, but she's physically healthy to attend the ball."

That was interesting. I wonder what was causing her to miraculously heal unlike anyone else. It was a puzzle for another time. "That's good news, Cal. It's good to know she's doing well. What about her brother?"

"He's healing – not as rapidly as Kim, but he's managing. I think that Dr. Corvaul might have miscalculated the amount of venom in her system. It would be a good reason for her healing faster than her brother. She never had an overly amount of poison in her system to begin with."

I began to snap the silver lining cuffs my father had given to me two years ago on, the metal shining in the last rays of sunlight that penetrated the room. "Good point. Either way I'm glad that she's better."

Cal stood from his perch, heading towards me. "You sure you're alright? I know this time of year is always-"

"I'm fine," I said forcefully. Cal stiffened, eyeing me warily. Taking a deep breath I said more calmly, "I just wish I could see her. But it's not feasible, and it's time that I stop hoping for things that are unattainable."

Calder clasped a hand on my shoulder, his eyes emitting compassion and understanding. It was the second time I've seen those two emotions inhabiting his person. For this, I would be eternally grateful to Kimberly. She had shattered his cold demeanor about the concept, and had shed light on the possibility of it in his life. It made him identify with what I have known all along.

"Maybe," Cal said slowly. "But what is life without hope, without a semblance of longing for the thing we want most? Sometimes, we have to fight for that desire instead of standing on the sidelines – watching others play the field and wanting what they have. Don't deprive yourself of life."

With those departing words, Cal left – the door closing behind him as the dull sound of his footsteps faded down the hall. I slumped down on the edge of my bed and glimpsed at my reflection in the mirror, seeing the half moon purple shadows under my eyes and the drastic cut of my cheeks under close examination.

Don't deprive yourself of life.

His words echoed in the dark void of my mind, becoming a broken record that I yearned to find and smash into a million pieces. But no matter how much I ached to flee and banish the words he'd uttered – deep inside I knew he was right.

Oh, how the tables have certainly turned.

Calder

With Kimberly's arm entwined in mine we entered the dining hall, meeting the elaborate and intricate display of brightly lit brass fixtures on top of marble columns, casting the vast space with its amber glow – while the beautiful glass chandelier hung in the middle of the room – the crystals shining brilliantly as the light caught the glass. The walls were covered from floor to ceiling in velvet plum drapes that enveloped the room with an exquisite and sophisticated atmosphere.

The distant sound of music the band played reached my ears as Kimberly tugged me towards the dance floor where others surrounded us, moving to the melody of the piano forte; the delicate notes forming a ballad.

I stepped in front of Kimberly, bowing as I asked, "May I have the honor of this dance, Miss Amato?"

She beamed, her crystal blue eyes shining behind the shimmering dark blue of her mask. Delicately she placed her hand in mine and said, "It would be my pleasure, Mr. Montgomery."

Placing my hand on the small of her back, I pulled her closer to me in a swift motion, closing the space between our bodies. Her cheeks flamed, but didn't pull away as I lead her in a dance. She followed effortlessly as we became one with the harmony – the music guiding us in a steady tempo. Our eyes locked to each other's, holding a fiery intensity that was only perceptible to us under the warm amber glow fixtures. It was as if everyone in the room disappeared and we were the only two people dancing to our own tune as we become lost in its melody.

The tempo of the music changed from slow and intimate to an exciting jazz beat, ending the magical spell that had been especially cast for the two of us. She began to pull away, but my heel stepped on the folds of her shimmering dark blue dress on accident.

Leaning forward I whispered in her ear, "Sorry. But I don't believe it's in my disposition to let you out of my sight." She shivered at the cool breath on her skin. As I pulled away, I saw the flush gracing her porcelain skin. Her hand was feverish hot when I grabbed it once again in mine, leading her in lively turns and woven dance steps that matched the composition. Her laughter at my effort lifted up my spirits as I plunged her into a dip, holding her there a second longer than necessary.

She giggled. "I'm impressed." I pulled her up and brought her close, pressing a lingering kiss on her lips. Her shoulders relaxed as I brought my hand and caressed the side of her cheek, feeling the warmth that radiated from her.

"Finally!" We both pulled away to look at an excited young girl in a flowing lavender dress, her eyes dancing with glee. "Well, it's about time."

It could only have been Beth and the guy next to her must have been Nole, his jade-green eyes shining behind the blue gem encrusted black mask. Kimberly smiled as I looped my arm around her small waist. "You guys having a good time?" I asked.

Beth nodded her heading enthusiastically. "It's amazing! I love the nineteenth century feel of this place. Everyone looks as if they've stepped out of an acclaimed movie set - costumes and all." She stopped, a thought surfacing in her mind as she looked around the room. "Where's Gabriel?"

"I have no idea," I said, stepping away from Kimberly to observe the room. How could I have easily forgotten about my best friend? My eyes swept the room until I detected a lone figure by a marble column, a drink idly in his hand. His gaze was set across the room and I followed it to the winding staircase only to see what had caught his attention.

In the middle of the stairwell was a glowing orb, floating seamlessly near a group of Keepers. They didn't seem to know that the light was there and went on with their conversation. But Gabriel saw it and he began to make his way towards it.

"Cal?"

I turned around to the sound of Kimberly's voice and saw that she was looking towards the staircase. "You found him, but where is he going?"

"I have no idea," I muttered. "Maybe he's going to get a breath of fresh air."

The idea quelled her curiosity and she turned back to converse with Beth and Nole. After a few minutes of glancing towards the staircase and seeing that there didn't seem to be any harm in the matter, I dropped it.

But there was still a hint of curiosity on my part as Gabriel disappeared from my sight.

Gabriel

I had been lazily watching the elegant clad dancers swirl in a mixture of deep purple hues and rich blue fabric, when at the corner of my eye I saw an unearthly bright light shining to my left. In an instant I knew that it was my ghost and as if it was calling my attention, it began to float away through the mass of bodies on the dance floor. There was no sign that anyone knew of the beautiful golden light among them as it made its way towards the staircase, hovering absentmindedly near a group of Keepers.

The light seemed to shine brighter as I watched. Before I knew it I was walking towards it, captivated by its mysterious beauty. I set my glass of champagne on a tray and in a haze followed the light up the staircase, and down the corridor. The shining light was the only available source of lighting in the otherwise dark hall. When the orb turned around a corner I was met with the vast darkness of the hall. In a swift motion I lit the torches among the wall, and continued to walk until I turned where I had last seen the beautiful unearthly glow.

My eyes fell upon an open room as I turned the corner. As I walked through the vacant room I saw a balcony overseeing the garden, but the light I had been following was nowhere in sight. Instead, there was a girl dressed in a flowing white Grecian style dress. Her hair fell loosely down her back in soft brown waves that shimmered where the moonlight caught some strands. As I approached, I saw that her hair was laced with specks of gold that matched a cuffed bracelet on her left wrist. The rich golden color reminded me of the unearthly light I had been blindly following a few moments before.

What's come over me?

The girl turned at the sound of my footsteps on the wooden floorboards, but I halted as I met her soft brown eyes hidden behind an intricate golden flecked white mask. Those eyes – they were beautiful, mysterious, familiar – yet, I was certain that I'd never seen her among the halls of the castle. I inhaled sharply as the strange familiarity crashed around me and time froze when I looked at the beauty before me. She was shorter than I was by a good two and her sun-kissed skin was like warm amber under the glow of the moon.

She was looking at me with curious eyes, and that's when I realized I'd been openly admiring her. Shuffling my weight from one foot to the other I said, "Sorry. I didn't mean to intrude."

I began to take a step back –never letting my eyes waver from hers – when her voice seized my departure.

"It's quite alright," she said politely. Her voice was like honey, sweet and familiar like a lost dream I barely remember. She tilted her head to the side and smiled, causing my heart to constrict. "I was just admiring the moon. It's quite beautiful tonight."

I looked up at the moon and saw that it was full, its light illuminating the world below. Slowly, I walked forward and stood beside her – gazing at the moon in comfortable silence. There was something painfully familiar about her as if I knew who she was, but at the same time I didn't have the slightest clue of her identity. Her mask hid her features except for her lips and eyes. She could be any of the hundreds of girls who lived here.

The one thing that didn't make sense was my easy comfort around her, which undoubtedly wasn't with many people besides our small makeshift group.

"What has brought you here?" She asked, softly. Her voice was sweet and held a trace of curiosity that lingered in the space between us. She was truly captivating and there seemed to be a magical spell woven around her, just like the beautiful light – strange that it had led me here, to her.

Had it been a possible sign?

"I was-" My voice caught in my throat as I became conscious of the truth on the tip of my tongue. What made me feel at peace around this mysterious girl? Was it the familiarity that seemed to surround her? Or was her hidden identity a cause for comfort? I was certain that she was not a Keeper or novice from this base. If she was neither then who was she?

"What's your name?" I asked instead – wanting to start somewhere to unravel the mystery that was her. She turned away from me, her eyes gazing down at the garden where only the white flowers were vibrant in the dark. I saw her shoulders stiffened, but then relaxed the next moment as she drew in a deep breath.

Her voice was soft and wistful when she said, "Melody. My name is Melody."

Her name was not one I recognized as I racked my brain for a face, but came up empty. She must be a guest brought from one of our Keepers, I thought. Turning to face her, I bowed before her in formal greeting with my hand outstretched for her to take. When I felt her small hand in mine I rose, bringing her hand to my lips, placing a kiss on her knuckles. Her gaze met mine under heavily lidded lashes, sending a tremor through my chest. Again, I questioned the emotions that this girl stirred within me; emotions that I believed had died long ago when I left Gwen behind.

"It's a pleasure to meet you, Mr. Montehue."

"Please, Mr. Montehue is my father. Call me Gabriel."

She let go of my hand and said, "Gabe-ree-all ," testing my name on her lips as if it was something she's never heard of before. Like something foreign and mystic from the ancients. Wait...how did she know who I was?

As if I'd uttered the question aloud she answered, "You're widely known for your accomplishments and hold the promise to go down in history as an exceptional courageous Keeper." Her voice was praising, but then it dropped to a teasing whisper – her eyes glistening in the moonlight. "That and you aren't wearing a mask."

Of course. The corners of my mouth twisted upwards into a smile. I should have known that without a mask anyone would know of my identity. I was like a black sheep in a herd of white ones; perceptible and unhindered in the wide open land.

Something she said caught my attention. It was like she knew what lied ahead in the near future. "I hold promise?" I asked, curiously – crossing my arms over my chest. "If I didn't know any better I would say that you are a Seer."

Melody's smile was radiant in the moonlight, her brown eyes dancing with a secret that I wanted to be a part of. I inched closer to her to the point that there were only a few inches between our bodies. I caught the strong scent of white lilies, and the warmth of the sun projecting from her very being. It was intoxicating – taking all myself control to not reach out and wrap my arms around her small frame.

There was some strong attraction pulling me towards her – overwhelmingly difficult to ignore. A glance in her direction indicated that it was the same for her by the tense set of her shoulders and the rapid beating of her heart.

Melody turned towards me, the expression on her face making my heart quicken inside my chest like an increasing metronome. There was sadness in her brown eyes as she said my name on her sweet lips. Her voice - it sounded so familiar, like a long forgotten song that had stopped playing for years. I knew her.

Where did I know her from?

She moved forward, closing the gap between us. The warmth that radiated from her scorched my skin in a way that a demon's poison never would be able to inflict. I inhaled the sweet aroma that could not be evaded from this beautiful, striking creature before me. Her eyes were tender and filled with fierce conviction when she said, "You will do extraordinary things in your lifetime. But getting there will prove to be a challenge with the highs and lows of life. Just remember one thing," she raised her hand and gently laid it upon my cheek. If I thought that her skin upon mine would burn I had been widely mistaken. It was soft as a flower's petal and warm as the sun shining on a spring day.

"Everything happens for a reason. The good, the bad – it all works together for a greater purpose. You will be an exceptional warrior in the future. Your fervor is what will make you great, but it will also be your weakness."

Slowly, she began to move away her hand from my cheek but I pressed it longer with my own – wanting to feel the calmness her touch ensued inside of me. Melody eyes widened, but she didn't protest. A soft sigh escaped her delicate lips as I wrapped my arm around her waist, bringing her closer to me. It was imperative that I have her near me, to breathe the sweet scent of her sun-kissed skin. Melody sank into my arms; a shiver ran down her spine as I tilted her chin and looked into her breathtaking eyes.

Her hand rested gently on my chest as I traced the online of her mask with my fingertips. Her skin was soft, and fragile just like a petal. My fear was that she would disappear into gold dust and this would have all been a dream – a beautiful, captivating dream.

"Gabriel!"

The sound of my name sent an electrical jolt between us, sending us reeling backwards with its invisible force. I exhaled a long breath that I had not been aware I was holding until that moment. Melody's breathing came out shallow, and I watched as she closed her eyes, taking deep soothing breaths to calm the beating of her racing heart.

Calder's urgent voice reverberated outside the French doors, and I let out an exasperated sigh. What could he possibly want? I debated whether I should stay here with Melody, and find the mystery that surrounded her. Or I could leave and figure out what Calder's emergency seemed to be.

Melody decided for me.

"You should go," she said in a huff. She gnawed at the bottom corner of her lip, pensively. Her eyes no longer held the tenderness that they had a few moments before. Urgency replaced the emotion as she said hastily, "Don't forget what I said."

"I-I," my voice was a low husky timbre as I fought for words to surface on my tongue. "I apologize for my-"

She turned her back to me and whispered something that was lost in the slight breeze that had begun to blow gently around us.

"Gabriel!" Calder's voice was closer and edged with hysteria. "Gabriel!"

I began to inch backwards towards the French doors, but there was a sinking feeling at the pit of my stomach. There was something about her that caused my heart to constrict inside of my chest. The only other person who had ever made me feel this way was...

"Gabriel, there you are-" I turned on my heel to a wide-eyed Calder, the French doors slamming against the wall at his entrance. "I've been calling your bloody name for-" He stopped, his eyes assessing mine and the area surrounding me. "What are you doing here by yourself?"

"Alone? I'm not-" I turned back around to introduce him to Melody, but she was gone. A frown makes its way on my lips as the sudden realization fills me with confusion and dismay. There was no trace to indicate that she ever was here or where she had gone.

Calder grabbed my shoulder and began to steer me through the room and out into the corridor. "What is the matter with you?" I shout, digging my heels to the ground. Anger penetrates through the confusion I feel, unleashing my resentment towards him for interrupting my time with Melody. "Why were you calling my name like-"

"Your father wants us," he said hastily. "He says it's important and that you need to come to the chamber immediately."

My eyebrows knit together as confusion once again floods the chambers of my mind - momentarily forgetting about the girl behind the mask. "What is it?"

He shook his head. "I don't know, Gabe" Calder resumed walking and I followed him down the corridor to the top of the staircase. "But he had a grieved look on his face when he told me to go find you. It can't be forthcoming."

EPILOGUE

G abriel

We entered the Council Chambers where my father was standing in front of a looking glass. Elder Montgomery was sitting in his chair along with the other council members. Their voices were in hushed tones as they shuffled papers and books to one another in frenzy. Calder left my side and joined his father, asking him in a low voice, "Why have you summoned us?"

"We have a mission for you…"

My father's hand clasped my shoulder, and I turned my attention to him, seeing the sympathy in his eyes. A tight grimace was set on his mouth as he said, "There's something you need to see. We just received a message of sorts."

"A message of sorts? What kind of message?" My voice was underlined with confusion and an edge of hysteria. Whatever the message was it couldn't contain good news – not by the way that everyone was acting. The Elders were speaking of a mission for Calder and most likely for me. I stopped listening to their conversation when I turned to see my father's solemn face. Wherever Calder went, I went. We were a deadly duo and seldom were assigned to a mission without the other.

"We don't know how this could have happened," Dad said slowly. "It's unusual and we need your full cooperation with this matter. Marrino will talk to you afterwards, understood?"

I nodded. His voice was cautious as if he was talking to a small child. What he was saying caused a quiver of fear to settle in the pit of my stomach. This was something that would matter to me. He was warning me to keep my emotions at bay because he knew me. He knew how I would react. But what could the matter be that he needed to warn me?

My question was answered when my father turned my attention to the looking glass as an image began to appear on its clear surface. At first it was foggy like a mist rolling onto the Yorkshire moors. Then it began to part as the image became clear, merging from gray fog to an amber glow sun setting on the horizon. I felt my father stiffen besides me as I folded my arms before me. I couldn't help but notice that the room had also become deadly silent. I glanced at Cal from the corner of my eye. He was watching me closely as if I was some sort of freakishly new speciman that had been discovered.

I gulped, feeling the uneasiness of the situation sink deeper into my very core. The image zoomed closer to a single car on the highway; it's main focus. There were other cars on the opposite end driving pass in normal speed. My thoughts were in disarray as I questioned the Council's motives for showing me a fragment of time. It was forbidden for a Keeper who wasn't of age to have a look at a different time; only the present was permissible to observe. The reason for this law was because the past or future was a delicate matter that should be dealt with care. If a time traveler went back to the past and changed an event – that event would have consequences. For every action there was an equal and opposite reaction. The same rule applied to the future.

A person could upset the very fabric of time when they changed the past. It was a concept we had been taught for years since we began our training; always treading with caution – it was dangerous ground.

There had to be a reasonable motive for it to be acceptable now – in this very moment.

When the image settled on the focal point – the person – I sucked in a sharp breath in surprise at seeing her paralyzed my body. I moved closer to the looking glass and reached my hand to trace the side of her beautiful sun-kissed face. It had been six years since I last saw her the day of my fourteenth birthday – the night I left her.

I turned to my father and saw his downcast eyes, his gaze avoiding mine. Something was definitely wrong. The room remained soundless as my eyes fell on the Elders with their solemn eyes and finally on Cal.

I'm sorry for what you're about to see.

His voice was full of sympathy in my mind. I tried to search his eyes for any indication of what he meant, but could only see compassion and remorse in his gray-blue eyes.

"Son," my father's voice brought my attention back to him. "Just watch. You need to see this."

Taking a deep breath, I turned my gaze back to the looking glass; prepared for whatever would happen.

Gwen was driving on the highway, listening to the low drone of a song on the radio. It was a normal day for her and saw the vague image of groceries in the back seat. Her beauty took my breath away as I noticed that her hair was longer than I remembered. It was also lighter from the sun, and wondered if she played a sport or spent hours laying lazily under the sun's rays. Her eyes were the same rich brown that I had grown to love. They were watchful and leveled as she drove; her attention solely on the wide expanse in front of her.

I longed to be with her, sitting next to her in the passenger seat. We'd talk about everything and nothing. Nothing would matter, but us in that moment of time. I had almost forgotten the unsettling feeling that had made a home in the core of my chest.

It was just an ordinary day.

Then the truck hit her.

Everything that followed was a blur.

The impact of the truck made her spin out of control and it flipped over the next moment. Her cries for help rang in my head like a blaring fire alarm that warned of a dire emergency. Instinct made me move forward, wanting to jump right through the looking glass to help her. But that wasn't possible. I couldn't do anything to save her.

I clenched my jaw as it pained me to watch her lost consciousness a few minutes afterwards. There was blood seeping through her royal blue t-shirt from the cut on her forehead. The focus of the image switched to the rear of the car where gas began to drip and pool in a steady-fast pace. After agonizing minutes of gruelingly watching, a spark was ignited catching on the pool of gas. The fire spread relentlessly, starting at the rear and finally making its deadly path to Gwen.

She didn't scream, she didn't stir from the black abyss. Her body was deathly still as the fire consumed her body in its fiery death. I sank to my knees, feeling my legs collapsed underneath me – no longer having the strength to stand.

Something had shattered within me as an excruciating pain clawed through my chest – my soul was being ripped away from me.

Calder

There were no words to describe the amount of anguish that Gabriel was going through after seeing the girl he loved die right before his eyes. No one knew what to do when he sank to his knees – his head cradled his hands as sobs racked his body in heart-wrenching spasms.

His emotions were intense, and I saw that my father was also being affected by Gabe's utter torment. He wasn't the only one. As I looked around the room, I saw the pity and sympathy in each of the Elder's eyes. Some couldn't even look at Gabriel – his pain too much to bear.

They didn't know how he felt – not even close.

But I did. His emotions were heightened that it was easy to read his thoughts (something that I hadn't done in a days because of a block he created). With his mental state fragile it was effortless to read the dismay and agony that settled over him like a dark foreboding aura. There was also blame. He blamed himself for what happened.

I took a seat down on the steps leading up to the dais. His pain flooded my mind and body in perpetual deadly waves on a stormy night. There was no telling how much time passed after Gabe's discovery of Gwen's death. Time was non-existent in the chamber, at least that's how it seemed. The next thing I realized was Marrino speaking to Gabriel asking him if he had anything of Gwen's that he could see. He instinctively clutched the silver chain around his neck, telling Marrino that he only had a gift she had given to him.

Marrino nodded saying, "That is enough."

Gabriel slowly removed the locket from his neck and held it in his hand for a moment before handing it to Marrino's outstretched palm. Marrino's hand closed around the locket, closing his eyes as he concentrated on the object.

After a few minutes, Elder Montehue inquired, "Do you see anything?"

"Yes," he whispered distantly. His forehead creased as his eyes strained close, setting his mouth in a firm grimace. "It's strange...she has more than one path; more than one fate. There are many paths her life could have taken, but only two are distinct."

Pushing myself up, I walked towards them – only to be stopped by Mr. Montehue's slight shake of his head. My brows furrowed in confusion, but I did as he commanded. I saw Marrino's eyes open wide as he regained focus of his surroundings. Gabriel vigilantly took the locket back from Marrino, closing his fist around the silver.

Mr. Montehue stepped away from his son and walked passed me with Marrino trailing behind. After they both settled into their seats, a low murmur settled over the seven members of the Council as decisions were discussed and finalized over the matter.

I heard Gabriel's tentative footsteps stop beside me – his blue-green eyes rimmed red from the strain of tears. He never once glanced my way as he watched the council, waiting for them to dispatch an order. What Gabriel didn't know was that I already knew what the next course of action would be. My father had told me first thing when we entered the chamber tonight.

"Calder," Elder Montehue said, acknowledging my presence. "Gabriel," we nodded in recognition and knelled – bowing our heads formally. "You may rise." Simultaneously, we stood erect as we waited for the Council's order.

I side-glanced at Gabriel and saw the tight set of his jaw, and the stiffness in his posture as he waited for his father's next words – the words that he would surely question against his better judgment.

"We have decided," Mr. Montehue began, "After careful con-sideration – we have decided that after a month of research in this particular case – Calder will be assigned to go back to the past."

"What?" Gabriel's voice was incredulous as if he had been told something that was inconceivable. "You aren't sending me back-"

"Gabe," Elder Marrino's voice interrupted his protests. When he spoke his tone was surprisingly compassionate and percep-tive; wistful in a way that could only be compared to man that once had gone through a similar situation as this. "We under-stand your love for this girl. It is the reason that we cannot allow you to join Calder on this particular mission. It's a conflict of interest and your feelings and thoughts may well obscure your judgment concerning this new development.

"Once we research her circumstance and gather further information, Calder will go back and decipher exactly what occurred to change her fate." Marrino's gaze settled on mine, adding, "You will tread carefully to not change significant events in her life. You'll have to work to lead her to the path where she marries and has a long and fruitful life rather than dying in that car crash. Is that clear?"

Gabriel was silent beside me like a stony statue incapable of emotion. His demeanor was just a mask to hide the depths of his reflections, but I knew what he was thinking and my father felt his torment like it was his own.

I finally nodded to Marrino's command. "I'll need to be informed on the details of this path you speak of, but I understand."

"You will be debriefed tomorrow," Mr. Montehue said wearily – sinking back into his chair. "If there isn't any more to add you may both be-"

Before Mr. Montehue could finish his sentence, Gabriel turned on his heel and insolently walked out of the chamber – the doors banging shut in a clamor at his departure. No one said a word at his brash behavior, and after a few minutes of silence I also took my leave.

Kimberly was waiting for me outside the chamber doors, leaning against the far wall of the hall. There wasn't a more gratifying moment in my life than seeing Kimberly waiting for me under the torch filled corridor. She ran, dropping her mask on the floor as she collided into my arms.

"I was so worried when you didn't come back. It's been hours. What happened? I saw Gabriel and he looked so distraught. I didn't know what to-"

"Shh..." I said soothingly into her hair, trying to calm her worries. "I've been given a mission. What time is it?"

She pulled back, her eyes roaming my own. "It's almost 3. What happened? What's wrong with Gabe?"

I sighed, clasping my hand at the back of my neck as the gravity of the situation finally sank in. My best mate's love of his life was dead. I was going back to save her life by leading her towards another man who she would eventually marry. All this was happening in a month. I had a month to gather additional information about Gwen's fate and death. One month to be with Kimberly before I left for an unknown amount of time back to the past.

Cradling Kimberly's hand in mine we walked down the corridor to the wing where our rooms were held. She was quiet and didn't ask any more questions – knowing in her heart that I would answer her questions when I was able. When we got to the door of her room she opened it and welcomed me inside. I sat down on her bed, leaning back on the headboard – my body finally feeling the effects of a prolonged day. She came to sit next to me as she kicked her black heels off her feet. I looped my arm around her shoulders, bringing her closer to curl up against the warmth of my body.

She let out a sweet and comforting sigh. She nestled her face into my chest, her nose pressed against my collarbone. After a few minutes of serene silence I finally told her everything.

I began with the story of Gabriel's unconditional love for Gwen – telling her of all the years that had separated them, yet his love forever burned for her like the eternal sun; never once wavering because of her absence. When I came to Gwen's death, I realized the absolute horror of what it would feel like to lose Kimberly as Gabriel had lost his one true love.

But it was Gwen's fate that I was going back to change.

I would go back to the past and prevent her death in order for her to live the life she was promised, and for Gabe to atone his guilt.

www.ingramcontent.com/pod-product-compliance
Lightning Source LLC
Chambersburg PA
CBHW070947190726
48292CB00004B/1370